DADDY SAYS

MAGGIE RYAN

Copyright © 2017 by Maggie Ryan

Published by Stormy Night Publications and Design, LLC.
www.StormyNightPublications.com

Cover design by Korey Mae Johnson
www.koreymaejohnson.com

Images by Period Images, 123RF/Sergiy Tryapitsyn, and 123RF/Nontawat Thongsibsong

All rights reserved.

1st Print Edition. December 2017

ISBN-13: 978-1981409716

ISBN-10: 1981409718

FOR AUDIENCES 18+ ONLY

This book is intended for adults only. Spanking and other sexual activities represented in this book are fantasies only, intended for adults.

CHAPTER ONE

What had she done to deserve such a gift? She'd have to thank Marcus, the maître d', for seating Mr. Lawson and his dinner companion at her station. Once she was at the table, she waited until there was a pause in their conversation, her greeting on the tip of her tongue when the man looked up. His eyes were the most amazing color she'd ever seen... a combination of the deepest turquoise of the Caribbean and the emerald green of moss found in a tropical rainforest. "Please, tell me I might serve you." It took the flash of his smile, the sound of a deep chuckle, and the heat she could feel flooding her face for her to realize what had just come out of her mouth. "Oh... I mean I'm here to serve..." She closed her eyes as if that would block out the reality that she couldn't seem to keep her foot out of her mouth. *God, I'm going to be so fired.*

"Look at me."

At the instruction, her eyes snapped open.

"Good, now take a breath."

"Huh?"

Mr. Lawson's chuckle had her flinching as she realized she obviously had not yet finished making a total fool out of herself. But the one who had spoken simply smiled and repeated his words.

"Just breathe. A nice deep breath." He took one himself as if to demonstrate how to follow his instruction and that did the trick. By the time he took his third, Jane was mimicking his actions. After another, he nodded.

"That's a good girl."

How could four little words make her feel like she'd achieved some goal, and his smile felt like she'd won some sort of award?

"It is my pleasure to serve... to wait on you... Fuck!"

The smile slipped from the man's lips, his dark head shaking a bit even as his eyes locked with hers again. "What is your name?"

No doubt about it. I'm going to lose my job because I just dropped an f-bomb in front of a customer. She fought the impulse to turn and run. *Breathe, idiot!* She needed to get herself under control immediately. Taking another deep breath, she smoothed her hands down her skirt and closed her eyes a brief moment before trying yet again. Unable to meet the man's eyes any longer, she turned to his companion. "Welcome back to Arturo's, Mr. Lawson. May I bring you something from the bar, or would you prefer to go ahead and order?"

"I'll have my regular," he said, his lips quirking a bit as if he was amused. The source of that amusement became clear when he added. "And, young lady, it would behoove you to answer Masterson's question before we go any further."

Did he say Master? Holy hell... he couldn't have. That title was not something bandied about in a public arena. Even as her head spun trying to keep her mind from going where it didn't belong, and to try to remember what question had even been asked, he leaned forward just a bit and spoke low as if to share a secret. "Oh, and I'd suggest an apology as well." He sat back, his lips curving into a smile. "Unless, of course, you are like my Michelle and prefer making your apologies after the fact."

"After? After what? Oh, after I get your drinks—"

"No, that's not what he means," Masterson corrected. "But that's not important at the moment."

"No? Oh, um… okay." Totally confused, she was about to turn away to bring their drink order when she realized she'd yet to get his. "Oh, what can I bring you, Mast…" No way she could get that word out, no matter if it cost her this job. "Sir."

His smile was back, and she couldn't blame him for being amused. She was acting like a silly teenager who was about to swoon over some impossibly handsome high school quarterback.

"You may bring me a Courvoisier neat. And, though no man could possibly deny the pleasure of hearing either title from your lips, my name is Sawyer Masterson."

Her face flamed again as he corrected her. No matter how kindly he'd put it, she was still making an ass of herself.

"I'm sorry… I'll get your drinks." Spinning away, she grimaced at the twinge that shot up her leg as her ankle twisted. Damn shoes! Only someone who never had to balance drinks and food on heavy trays would choose such ridiculous footwear. But seeing as it was unlikely that Arnold Arturo, the owner of the expensive restaurant, had ever worn anything more restrictive than his custom-made shoes along with his tailored suits, he'd have no idea how much her feet ached by the end of her shift. It was her job, along with every other woman he employed, to project a certain image. Their uniform of pleated black skirts that brushed the top of their knees, white blouses unbuttoned just enough to draw an eye but not be considered trashy, and four-inch black stilettos was meant to convey refined elegance.

At the bar, she placed the drink order, a bit astonished she actually remembered it. Wishing she could bend over and rub her ankle, but knowing to be caught would be frowned upon, she placed all her weight on her right foot and slowly rotated her left, wincing at the sting.

"How's it going?"

Jane glanced up to see Sarah and gave a soft groan that had nothing to do with her ankle. Just beyond her friend, Jane could see her boss was approaching the table she'd just left. She knew he was about to get an earful about the awful service she was giving. "Let's just say, I'll most likely be looking for another job."

Sarah looked back toward the dining room. "Uh oh, that doesn't sound good. What happened?"

"What didn't?" Jane said and then sighed. "Have you ever had a customer who makes you so nervous you can't even remember your name?" Before Sarah could answer, Jane groaned. "Shit. That's what he asked me! God, he must think I'm a total moron." She went on to fill Sarah in on how she'd stumbled over her words and made an idiot out of herself. "So, as I said, it's been nice working with you."

Sarah smiled and turned her attention back to Jane, reaching over to pat her hand. "I can see why you might be a bit flustered. That is one incredibly handsome hunk. I can think of all sorts of ways to service him." Jane groaned and Sarah laughed. "Relax. I'm sure you're overreacting. Just sashay over there, give him one of your smiles, and bat those long eyelashes. By the time he pays the check, I'll bet you'll find a nice fat tip to thank you for all your personal… service."

Jane could feel her face heat even as she slapped Sarah's hand away. "Ha, ha, very funny. I just hope he is as forgiving as he is handsome." Picking up the silver tray that held her customers' drinks, she gently set her foot down, grateful that it felt as if her ankle would hold her without too much discomfort. Taking her first step, she had to fight not to flush yet again when Sarah gave another piece of advice.

"Oh, and another button undone would go a long way to having him forget his own name. I really would hate to have to find another roomie."

Jane didn't bother to answer. She would give the best service she could as she really couldn't afford to lose her job. Not when she was so close to reaching her goal. She approached the table, her attention on the glasses on her tray. Looking up, she almost stumbled again, the liquor sloshing a bit in the glasses as the tray shook in her hands. The man who would most likely be handing her her last paycheck was still talking with her customers. Well, she couldn't just stand there, and as much as she wanted to knock back both drinks herself, until she got fired, she had a job to do. Slapping a smile on her face, she approached the table, incredibly relieved when her boss stepped away, giving her a smile and a nod... not the look of 'your ass is grass' that she had expected.

She placed a thick white napkin down at each place. "Johnnie Walker, three ice cubes," she said, setting the heavy crystal rock glass containing the scotch down first. She hoped that by bringing Mr. Lawson his preferred brand, he'd remember she wasn't usually so... so flustered. Picking up the snifter, her hand shook just a bit as she placed it on the other napkin. "Your cognac."

"Thank you."

Lifting her eyes, she met his. "You're very welcome, Master... I mean, Mr. Masterson." Damn it! What was it about this man that had her twisting her words?

"That's quite all right, Miss..."

Forget Sarah's prediction, she was the one who'd forgotten her own name... again. Her breath caught in her throat as his hand lifted toward her. When his fingers touched her, she gasped, her nipples tightening instantly even though he wasn't touching her breasts. Instead, he was brushing her hair back, and as she stared down at his hand, she not only saw her blouse did not hide the effect of his touch, but she also saw the oval tag pinned to the fabric. He wasn't attempting to cop a feel—he was simply reading her nametag.

"Oh—my name, um, it's Jane... Jane Knight."

"It's a pleasure to meet you, Jane," he said, dropping his hand and wrapping his fingers around the bowl of his glass, lifting it and giving it a swirl. "It's a very pretty name."

Jane watched as he lifted the snifter to his mouth, inhaling the aroma of the expensive brandy before allowing the first sip to pass his lips. Realizing that she was actually running the tip of her tongue along her bottom lip, she instantly pulled it back inside her mouth. "Um... thanks."

"Sir."

"Excuse me?" Turning her head, she addressed Mr. Lawson. Why did she feel he was chastising her? What was she missing? He leaned a bit toward her.

"Respect. Manners go a long way in seeking forgiveness."

Manners? Forgiveness? What was that supposed to mean? She turned back to Mr. Masterson, suddenly wondering why she felt so out of her element. "I'm... um, thank you, sir. I don't know what..."

"Relax, Jane. Edward tends to be a bit grumpy when he's separated from his wife for too long. You're doing fine."

Jane could picture a very pretty woman who often dined with Mr. Lawson. "Oh, I hope your wife isn't ill?"

Edward chuckled. "No, she might not be feeling very well right now, but it's not due to sickness. But, thank you for your concern."

His response didn't make a great deal of sense to Jane, but she didn't know what else to say. "Well, I do hope she feels better soon." Turning back to Mr. Masterson, she said, "Thank you, sir, I appreciate your kindness," she said, again feeling a ridiculous pleasure at his words. "I don't know why I'm... well, I'm usually not so..." At his smile, she felt a fluttering in her stomach, not able to voice the reason why she was so flustered as she truly didn't understand it herself.

"Are you ready to take my order?"

"Your order?" It took her a second to remember her duties before she gasped. "Oh, for dinner. Of course, I mean, yes, sir. What would you like?"

"The wedge salad, prime rib and... which would you recommend, the baked or mashed potatoes?"

"Either is an excellent choice, but the mashed does

contain a lot of garlic in case you… uh… either is great!" As his eyebrow quirked again, she grimaced. Great, he'd think she either was giving him a warning about some talisman to keep him safe from a vampire attack or that he might want to consider his breath in case he planned on kissing anyone after dinner. A wish that he'd choose to lock lips with her had her cheeks heating and her pulse racing.

"Good advice. I'll take the baked potato."

She took Mr. Lawson's order as well and then turned away, trying to walk without limping to the kitchen where she could finally attempt to pull herself together.

CHAPTER TWO

"Sawyer, you are going to give the poor girl a stroke."

"Me? I'm not the one dropping innuendoes," Sawyer Masterson said, watching as the young woman practically ran across the floor, noticing her wince and the slight hop as she pushed through the door. Had she injured herself in those ridiculous heels? His fingers flexed as he imagined pulling her onto his lap, reaching down to remove the shoe, and then massaging her trim ankle.

"Sawyer? Sawyer?"

Looking across the table, he saw Edward grinning. "What?"

"You didn't hear a word I said, did you? What are you thinking about?"

Sawyer shrugged. "Nothing in particular."

"Bullshit. I'm willing to bet that you're wondering about little Jane. You can't tell me that you missed how she barely kept herself from falling to her knees before you."

"Is she why you chose this particular restaurant? I've told you before, I really don't need any help—"

"Double bullshit. If you weren't interested in finding your own Little, you never would have contacted the agency. Face it, it's not easy to find the perfect mate, and it's nothing to be ashamed about in seeking a bit of help. Our proclivities aren't those of most men and put the majority of women out of the running from the get-go."

Sawyer glanced toward the door where Jane had disappeared. "I realize that you believe you have some sort of sixth sense, but the odds of this working out are pretty astronomical."

Edward grinned. "People do win the lottery, you know. Besides, Miss Knight practically glows with the need to serve, and I don't mean drinks and food. Don't be an ass, Sawyer. You've not been able to keep your eyes off her since the moment we walked in. Even if it winds up she is not the one, at least you won't kick yourself because you never even offered her the choice."

Sawyer couldn't deny he'd felt something from the moment he'd watched the young woman approach their table. On the outside, she ticked every one of his boxes. She was petite, her black hair was long and wavy, her eyes were the color of violets and that tongue… he'd only seen the very tip, but when she'd run it along her bottom lip, his cock had hardened at the thought of her kneeling before him, eyes shimmering with tears from the punishment he'd just delivered for her cursing, and her mouth obediently opening when instructed, her sweet tongue ready to lick along his shaft as she performed her penance. Fuck, even thinking about how it would feel having the warm wetness of her mouth engulfing him had his cock twitching again.

Edward's chuckle had his head jerking back to his friend. "Face it, you're a goner." He nodded toward the door, and Sawyer turned to see Jane slowly walking toward them, a huge tray balanced on one shoulder. When his instinct was to jump up, relieve her of the burden while scolding her for carrying something far too heavy, he knew Edward was correct. The only thing remaining was to see if his initial reaction about Jane's fumbling over her words, the address she blushed after saying, and her offer to serve meant she was a natural submissive. There was only one way to find out.

Though he ate the food set before him, his main attention was on Jane. She seemed to have gotten better control of herself as she served her other customers. And yet whenever he caught her eye, she'd instantly lower her gaze as her cheeks pinkened. At the end of the meal, she offered them coffee and dessert, and though not a man who frequently indulged in sweets, he asked what she'd recommend.

"Our pastry chef is a genius," she said with obvious pleasure. "Anything he offers is wonderful. I'll bring you the tray—"

"That's not necessary. Just bring me whatever is your favorite and a coffee, black."

"Yes, sir," she said, the blush again blooming up from her neck to settle in her cheeks. All he could think about was how her nether set of cheeks would look with a pink blush put there by his hand.

He didn't have to look across the table to know that Edward was enjoying himself immensely. The men had known each other for years and shared a great deal of the same interests. Hell, they'd discovered the fact that they preferred their women submissive while in college and had gone on to learn that they each wanted a woman who, though adult, desired to be allowed to retreat into childhood when life became overwhelming. A woman who gave control over to their chosen dom or, as it was called in their lifestyle, their 'daddy.'

With the arrival of a huge, seven-layer piece of chocolate cake, he knew that Jane had a sweet tooth. Her smile showed her pleasure as she set it down before him. "There is a raspberry purée between each layer and the dark chocolate ganache icing is simply to die for." His laugh had her eyes meeting his and for the first time, she joined in his amusement with a giggle that had his cock lengthening yet again. "I know, I sound silly, but I promise, it is the most sinful thing on earth."

"Really?" At her nod, he grinned and quirked his eyebrow. "It looks absolutely delicious, I agree, but, little one, I can think of far more sinful things to enjoy."

Her gasp and widening of her eyes, her nipples almost jumping to attention, and the fact that he could swear he could detect the scent of her arousal made his next move so very easy. Never taking his eyes from her, he filled his fork with a bite of the dessert and lifted it... not to his lips, but to hers.

"Open." If ever she asked how he'd known she would be his, he'd be able to state the exact moment. Her instant obedience, her acceptance of the bite, the closing of her lips around the tines of the utensil, and her softly uttered moan of pleasure would forever be imprinted on his brain.

"Good girl," he softly praised, sliding the fork from her mouth. When her tongue made a reappearance, licking along her lip, his cock turned into a steel rod. Wishing he could be tasting something far more enticing, he took a bite of cake. Swallowing, he nodded. "Excellent choice, Jane. It is delicious."

"I... I'm glad, sir." The moment was broken when a crash and the sound of breaking glass rang out. He watched her as she jerked back a step, her eyes scanning the table as if expecting that she'd caused the commotion.

"Relax, little one. It wasn't you."

"Oh... good. Um, I'll... I'll bring you the check." Not waiting to hear if that would be acceptable, she spun away and was soon out of sight.

Sawyer set down his fork. The pleasure had been in watching her enjoy it. Picking up his coffee cup, he took a sip and shook his head as Edward remained silent, though Sawyer knew it was killing the man. "Fine, you are right. She seems perfect."

"I'm far too refined to tell you, 'I told you so,' but, well, I told you so," Edward said, finishing his piece of cheesecake and sitting back. "I've done my part. The rest is up to you. Use the card, Sawyer. I have no doubt you won't be disappointed."

Within moments, Jane was back, placing the leather bill folder onto the table. "I hope you enjoyed your evening. It was my sincere pleasure to... to serve you."

"And it was mine to have you do so," Sawyer said. She blushed, nodded, and turned away. He pulled his wallet from his jacket. After using the pen provided, he slipped some bills inside the folder before closing it. As he stood, he could never remember a single time in his life when he had been more reluctant to call it a night. Still, he knew that Edward was only partially correct. The rest wasn't up to him... it would be up to Jane.

CHAPTER THREE

Jane sighed. She'd seen Mr. Masterson fingering a card and had thought she'd get another chance to linger… if only for a moment when she returned the credit card slip to him. Instead, she watched the men until they'd disappeared and then approached the table. Picking up the folder, she flipped it open. Instead of the credit card she'd expected, she saw a sheaf of bills. Closing it, she moved toward the kitchen where she'd enter the sale. It had gotten late and there was a line at the register.

Sarah joined her, two folders in her hands. "So, do we need to scrounge the dumpster for boxes to pack your stuff?"

"Geez, you're supposed to be my friend, not ready to kick me to the curb," Jane mock complained, bumping her hip against Sarah's when her friend only laughed.

"You know I'm kidding. You were just so positive you were going to get canned."

Finally reaching the register, Jane lifted the stack of bills, causing Sarah's eyes to widen. "Holy shit, what did they order? That's a lot of money."

Jane was a little surprised as well. The bills not only covered the check, which was far more than she'd ever be able to afford for a meal, though far less than she'd seen paid in Arturo's, but it would be the largest tip she had ever earned. About to slide the money into the register, she saw something slip out and fall to the floor. Bending, she picked it up. She'd been right. She had seen a black card... but it was not a black American Express card.

"What is that?" Sarah asked, leaning forward as if to see better.

"I don't know," Jane admitted, her fingertip sliding across the front of the card. It was the size of a credit card and almost as stiff as plastic. And yet, those were the only similarities. Instead of a customer's name, only one word was written in a beautiful script across the face. Frowning a bit, she noticed that an address of a website ran in block print across the bottom of the card. It still made no sense to her, but she felt a tingle run through her as she looked down at the pink script. *Favored.* What did that mean?

"Jane, hurry up. I'd like to get home," another server in line called.

"Oh, sorry, Karen," she said, sliding the card into her pocket. Finishing her transaction, she moved away only to barely miss bumping into her boss. "Sorry," she muttered again.

"I just wanted to commend you, Miss Knight. Mr. Masterson made it a point to inform me that your service was exemplary this evening."

"He did?"

Mr. Arturo smiled. "Yes, Miss Knight, he did. Keep up the good work."

"I will. Thank you, sir."

"You're welcome." As he walked away, Jane wondered how addressing her boss as sir gave her absolutely no tingling feeling, no sense of expectation or excitement. But addressing a man she'd just met with the same word had caused her entire body to thrum.

"You about ready to go?" Sarah asked. Though the restaurant didn't close for another half-hour, neither of them had an occupied table.

"Sure, let's see if there's anything left to eat." Mr. Arturo might like to give off the vibe of being a hard ass, and he was when it came to demanding the very best of his employees. But, he was also a nice man. Besides donating generously to various food banks in the area, he also allowed his employees to take home food that had not been served, rather than to have it thrown away. The two women thanked the chef as they accepted the bag containing lasagna, salad, and breadsticks.

"Wait up," Brian called. "Here, dessert is on me tonight."

"Thanks, you're a doll!" Sarah said, accepting another container, this time showing her appreciation in a far more personal way by giving his cheek a kiss. Peeking inside, she said, "Yum, I love cheesecake."

Though it wasn't Jane's favorite, she discovered she was rather glad there was no slice of chocolate cake inside. She doubted that if there had been she would have been able to enjoy it anywhere near as much as she had that one single bite that Mr. Masterson had fed her himself. Sliding her hand into her pocket, she fingered the card. The first chance she had, she'd be logging on to the website to see why this card had been left for her.

• • • • • • •

"Damn it! Why give me a card when I can't access the freaking website!" Staring at the laptop's screen, she erased the address she'd typed in and tried again. The same result came up. The only thing that appeared was a black screen with the same pink script and the same word, *Favored*. Below it was a box where she supposed some sort of access code was to be entered. Screw that, she had no idea what to even try.

Sighing, she leaned back against the stack of pillows she'd piled up against her headboard and closed her eyes.

Somehow she knew that she was meant to figure this out. She had not given exemplary service, not from the way she'd stumbled over her words and acted like she'd never waitressed before, but still, he hadn't seemed like the type of person who would pull some sort of joke in retribution. No, he seemed like the sort of man who would... Jane could feel her heart beat a bit faster and her tummy flutter as her thoughts took her to a place she'd been avoiding ever since he'd given her a look of disapproval when she'd dropped the f-bomb.

He might not be one to pull a prank, but she had no doubt that he was a man who wouldn't hesitate to punish a naughty girl. *Naughty girl? Where did that come from? I'm not a girl, I'm a grown woman. Yeah, a grown woman who spends far too many hours reading those books on my Kindle and fantasizing about being one of those characters, one of those sassy girls who finds the man of her dreams... a big, strong, stern man who swears to love and protect her.* She squirmed a bit as a scene from the latest book she'd read flashed across her mind's eye. *A man who gives a shake of his head, sends his girl the 'look,' and then informs her that she'd be going to bed with a very hot bottom.*

Good grief, she needed to get a grip! Those characters weren't real and those scenes were fiction. Life was not an erotic fairytale! Instead of letting her imagination run wild, she needed to try to find the freaking access code!

She forced her mind back to the problem at hand. Okay, if it wasn't a joke, what was it? Some sort of puzzle... a test? And if so, what was she missing? Her thoughts ran back across the evening, and her body instantly reacted when she remembered how his fingers had brushed her hair back. Her nipples tightened and she felt her panties becoming a bit damp. Damn, she'd only just changed into clean ones after her shower. What would it feel like to have his fingers touching her body, thumbing her nipples, sinking into her slick... Whoa! Snapping her eyes open, she sat up. That path would not have her solving the puzzle.

Picking up the card, she stroked it, the embossed

lettering seemingly giving weight to the word... like it was important. That the person owning the card was somehow special. Her eyes widened. Could it be that simple? Moving her mouse, she clicked it on the box. Her fingers hovered over the keyboard for a moment before she sucked her bottom lip between her teeth and typed in Mr. Masterson. No new screen opened when she hit enter. Okay, maybe it wasn't so formal. Typing in the name Sawyer Masterson had her holding her breath and then exhaling loudly when absolutely nothing happened. Crap. Didn't websites lock someone out when too many incorrect attempts to enter were made?

Come on, think. Why would he leave the card for me unless he wanted me to access this site? She chewed on her lip for a moment and then smiled as she considered the thought she'd just had. Who was holding the card? *She* was. Entering her name, she gave a squeal of victory when the screen slowly began to change, only to groan when another text box appeared.

Leaning forward, she read the words on the screen.

Welcome, Jane. You are favored. Please enter the password given to you by the one who has chosen you.

"Welcome, my ass," Jane muttered. "Whatever happened to a simple, 'I'd like your number so I can call you'? This is all a bit too *Mission Impossible* if you ask me."

"What are you mumbling about?" Sarah suddenly asked, dropping onto the bed next to her. Jane slammed the lid of her laptop closed, shocked that she hadn't been aware of her roommate entering.

"Nothing."

"Liar, liar, pants on fire," Sarah said. "Anybody who closes a computer that fast is definitely looking at things she shouldn't be." She nudged Jane aside in order to sit right next to her, sharing the mound of pillows. Handing her a fork, Sarah held out the plate that contained the slice of cheesecake.

Jane put a bite on her fork, wishing it was being offered

to her by Master... *MasterSON!*

"Oh, man, that sounded more like an 'I'm so horny' than a 'this is good cheesecake' moan." Reaching out with her own fork, Sarah tapped the cover of the computer. "Come on, we're both big girls, and it's been a while. I could use a good porn video myself."

"It's not porn," Jane said, shaking her head. "Hell, to be honest, I have no idea what it is."

Sarah picked up the card. "Does it have something to do with this?"

Resisting the urge to snatch it out of her friend's hand, Jane nodded, sighed, and opened the computer again. "I finally figured out the first screen but now am stuck at this one. I'm telling you, I've never seen a site so difficult to access. You don't suppose he's some sort of government agent trying to coerce me into breaking all sorts of laws, do you?"

Sarah laughed. "You watch far too much TV, girl. If that were the case, this card would have already self-destructed. So what happened when you entered the password?"

"Nothing as I have no flipping clue as to what it can be!" Jane said, taking another bite of the dessert.

"Did you try SawyerMasterson1007?"

Jane looked at her as if she'd lost her mind. "*I* watch too much TV? Who are you, Bond... Jamie Bond? Geez."

"Go ahead, what have you got to lose?" Sarah teased, pointing to the screen. "If I'm right, you have to clean the entire house including windows, baseboards, and the bathrooms."

"Fine," Jane said, typing the code in only to huff. "I can't believe I even thought that might work. Looks like you'll be the one scrubbing toilets, Ms. Moneypenny."

"You typed it wrong. Get your mind off Ian Fleming. I said 1007, not 007."

"Whatever." A few clicks later, Jane's tune changed. "Oh, my God! How did you know that?" A sinking feeling had her eyeing her friend. "Please don't tell me that you and he… that you both…"

"Oh, no," Sarah said. "Honey, I would never do that to you. Friends don't let their friends go out with ex-boyfriends."

"Then how do you explain knowing the password?"

"Easy," Sarah said, laying the card down. "He wrote it on the back."

Jane groaned. She'd never even looked at the back of the card.

"Whoa, are you actually considering this?" Sarah asked, her brow furrowing as she sat back against the pillows again.

"Considering what?" Jane asked, taking her eyes off the card.

"I honestly thought this was some sort of exclusive dating site, but I've never seen anything like this."

Jane studied the screen and had to admit she hadn't either. She'd sort of been expecting a dating site as well, but this seemed far more than that. It wasn't asking for her favorite restaurant or wine. It wasn't asking what her idea of a perfect date would be. Hell, it wasn't even asking her if she preferred blond or dark-haired men. There was only an instruction on the screen.

In order to continue, you agree to grant Master Masterson remote access to your computer. He will assist you in completing the questionnaire found on the following pages. If you choose not to continue, or terminate the session before the final agreement has been signed, the opportunity will be closed.

Below the note there were two boxes. Choosing one would grant him access. Clicking on the other would end the session.

"Wow! I wouldn't have pegged him as some sort of IT nerd."

Sarah snorted. "Seriously? That's what you get from this screen?"

"Sure, I mean, I don't know how to do that," Jane said. "Hey, how does he even know I'm logged on right now?"

"Honey, sometimes I wonder about you." Sarah reached

toward the screen, her finger tapping against one word. "Forget nerd, your guy considers himself a master, and I'm guessing the moment you accessed the website, he was informed. The real question is what sort of questions does he want you to answer, and why does he wish to watch while you do?"

"I don't know. Maybe he wants to know if I'd like to go out with him or something," Jane said.

Sarah gave her a long look. "Jane, you need to give this some serious thought. I know the man had some sort of... effect on you, but, this isn't just dating. Anyone who is to be addressed as Master is not going to be offering just dinner and a movie. Are you ready to share your fantasies, your desires? Are you prepared to dig deep and answer intimate questions?"

"How do you know they are going to be those sorts of questions?"

Rolling her eyes, Sarah said, "Think about it. This is not some sort of tame matchmaking site. You can't even access it without a card and a code. You are a 'favored' one, and the man addresses himself as Master. It's not a huge leap to make to understand that this is some sort of seriously heavy BDSM hook-up site."

"So you think I should say no?"

"I'm not saying that. I'm just saying that you need to think about what you are expecting and what you are willing to offer in return because I assure you, you will be offering something." She looked at the screen again and smiled. "But, I will say that while it's a little scary, it's also intriguing. Sort of like skipping all the bullshit and getting right to the heart of the matter."

"What would you do?"

Giving her a hug, Sarah scooted off the bed. "I'd follow my heart."

After her friend left the room, Jane sat for a long time considering Sarah's words. When she found herself stroking the card, she had her answer. She'd spent her entire twenty-four years looking for something that she'd never managed to find. She'd had boyfriends in her youth and even a few relationships she'd thought might go somewhere. Yet, not a single person had ever had her body heating and her heart pounding as this man had with nothing more than a look and a few words shared. Jane knew Sarah was right; she would be expected to offer something. Every cell in her body seemed to be alive, filling her with the infinite possibilities she had only read about, but had yearned to explore. It might be a little unusual—okay, it definitely fell in the crazy department—but she'd never be able to live with herself if she didn't take a chance. Besides, even in BDSM play, weren't there supposed to be strict rules to follow and safewords to stop all action if she found she couldn't handle whatever it was that her master desired?

Biting her lower lip, she imagined looking into those incredible eyes and asking, "What should I do, Master?" His answer was absolutely clear. With one little click of her mouse she made her choice. As the screen changed again, she could swear she heard him saying "that's my good girl," and she knew her life was about to change.

CHAPTER FOUR

Sawyer took another sip of his cognac, his eyes on the screen before him. The fact that Jane had accessed the website not long after she'd gotten off work had him very pleased. He had questioned his use of the agency but, with Edward's, as well as other friends' testimonies, he'd finally acquiesced. But that had been months ago. It was not until tonight that he'd found a woman he'd instantly considered as favored. It was a rather archaic word and yet, it seemed to fit not only how he'd felt, but it fit Jane Knight. She had an air of innocence that tugged at him, that had him wanting to teach her things she'd most likely never considered.

His brow furrowed as he checked his watch. While it had taken Jane a while to ascertain the access code and password, it seemed to be taking quite a bit longer for her to continue. His fingers itched to use the keyboard, but until he was granted permission, he had to wait and patience wasn't exactly his forte. Not when it pertained to something he'd been waiting to happen for a long time.

"Come on, sweetheart. Don't be frightened. Click the button and let's begin our journey."

A few moments later, he smiled as the woman who had somehow instantly become important to him made her choice. Not wanting to make her wait, he set down his glass and began to type.

Jane, Thank you. I am pleased to see you've discovered that I think you are a very special young lady. As you continue on your journey, know that it will be my greatest pleasure to be with you every step of the way.

The following screens will contain a list of questions that only you and I will have access to. I imagine you will find the first no more invasive than ones you'd fill out to apply for a job. The next few will serve to provide some information about your past. The final pages will be far more personal. Know that these are not meant to embarrass or judge you. They are simply a means to allow me to formulate a plan for your exploration of what I sincerely hope will be exactly what you've wanted, what you've dreamed about and have yet to find. There are no right or wrong answers, and I have no preconceived expectations.

You'll find that I abhor dishonesty, and, yes, I consider omission to be a lie. As I also believe in complete disclosure, let me be clear. This is not some matchmaking service. I am not interested in dating to see if we are compatible. I already know that we are and believe that you feel the same. Will some of the questions make you uncomfortable… yes. Will some make you blush… I have no doubt they will, and might I say that I find the fact that you blush so easily absolutely adorable.

Will some have you squirming… most likely if you choose to answer dishonestly and I later discover you've fibbed. There are consequences for naughtiness. Misbehavior will have you paying a price that will vary depending on the infraction, but will always include making your apology over my knees, or bent over a bed, a chair, the arm of a couch, offering your bare bottom knowing I will indeed make it burn.

Take your time answering as this is a serious step that you are taking. I realize I am asking a great deal… but know that I am committed to guiding you, to disciplining you, and to teaching you all about the pleasures and joy found in submission. I am asking for your honesty and your trust. I promise, I will treasure each and never abuse either.

With anticipation,

Sawyer Masterson

• • • • • • •

Holy hell! Jane felt as if she were on an emotional rollercoaster as she read the screen for a second time. The words made her feel both excitement as well as trepidation. It was exactly as Sarah had said... he wasn't asking her out on a 'date'. By answering whatever questions were to follow, he was basically skipping several dates where a couple gradually learned more about each other. But was that such a bad thing? She'd dated men before and, even after several weeks, she hadn't truly known them or felt they knew her true self. She had no idea how this man had been able to exchange only a few words and had managed to discover one of her deepest, darkest secrets. All she knew was that from the moment he'd met her eyes, she'd been lost.

Reading the note again, her eyes lingered on the section about offering her bottom... her bare bottom for his punishment. She'd not truly considered that as something common in a D/s relationship. But then, since she'd never actually been in such a dynamic and only had her fantasies to go by, perhaps it was more standard than she'd thought. Realizing that her buttocks were clenching and her heart racing, she knew she had so much to learn. Maybe it was a good thing to cut to the chase. Still, he would know so much about her and she'd know what? Nothing really... he wasn't answering any list of questions.

He'd said to take her time, and she was going to take him up on that offer. Sliding off the bed, she left her bedroom in search of Sarah... or more precisely, Sarah's computer.

"May I borrow your laptop?" Jane asked as she entered the living room.

Sarah looked up from the book she was reading. "Something wrong with yours?"

"No, but I'm afraid that if I change windows, I'll screw up the questionnaire."

"Ah, so there really are questions? What is he asking?"

"I don't know yet. I haven't gotten that far, but I want to look something up," Jane said.

"Something or someone?" Sarah asked with a grin.

"All right, I want to google him. Is that an awful thing to do?"

"Hell, no, I think that's a great idea," Sarah said, tossing her book aside. "And smart." She grabbed her laptop and soon a photo of Sawyer Masterson was on the screen.

"Wow, that's a lot of sites," Jane said, looking at the lists available that contained some sort of information on Sawyer.

The two continued to click and read snatches about Sawyer's life. Jane had thought he must be a man of means, but she'd had no idea that he was the owner of a corporation and employed several hundred people.

"He's very successful, isn't he?" Jane asked.

"If by successful you mean rich, yeah, I'd say that's a fact. I've heard of Masterson Enterprises, but didn't connect it with your guy. Hey, there he is with Mr. Arturo."

Jane saw the photo of her boss and his wife at some sort of fundraiser he'd chaired, but her eyes went to the man beside them. It seemed that he was quite generous as well, presenting Mr. Arturo with a $100,000.00 check to help feed the hungry in the city.

From their searching, they learned that Sawyer was thirty-six, had never married, was a sports fan, and appeared as a regular donor at various charity events.

"Well, girl, I have to say, it seems he's not only legit, he's a good guy," Sarah said and then sighed.

"What?"

"Don't mind me. I'm just wondering when I'm going to meet someone who thinks I'm a favored one."

Jane reached over and gave her a hug. "I'm pretty sure Brian sees you that way, and you'll always be my favorite."

Sarah hugged her back and then gestured toward the book she'd tossed onto the coffee table. "Not for long.

Listen, I've seen your Kindle and know we share a love for the same sort of books."

Jane felt her face flame as the words from her screen popped into her head. "True, but, what if that's all I can handle? You know, reading about it. I'm not sure I actually want to... well, experience those things."

Sarah laughed. "Jane, don't ever play poker. The other players will wipe you out. You can't lie to save your life. You've been looking for a man who will not only love you like you deserve, but keep you on your toes. If this man isn't saying that he will teach you exactly what he expects, and guide you along the way, then I say don't bother." She paused and then added, "Am I right? Do you already have a feeling that Mr. Hunky will be able to meet your needs?"

Releasing the lip she'd been gnawing on, Jane nodded. "I don't already 'feel' it; he practically said those exact words."

Sarah pulled Jane to her and squeezed. "I thought so, and, damn, girl, I'm really happy for you! I'm really thrilled that you finally might have found the perfect guy."

Jane knew she was telling the truth. The women had been friends since the first day Jane had begun work at Arturo's. They had been there for each other in good times and bad and were each other's strongest supporter. "Thanks, Sarah. Um... would you still feel the same if I tell you that he also said that there will be a price to pay for... misbehavior?"

Sarah canted her head to the side, her brow furrowing a bit. "What sort of price?"

Feeling her buttocks clenching again, Jane took a moment, thinking how to put it and decided the truth was the only way. "He said I'd be expected to present my bottom... my bare bottom and he'd make it burn."

A grin replaced the questioning look on Sarah's face. "I've always wanted to know what it's really like to be restrained to one of those spanking benches in those books. I swear, it just makes me quiver."

"He didn't mention restraints or spanking benches, but, well, he did mention being over his lap or bent over a bed. It sounded more like... well, how a naughty child is punished instead of some sexy submissive," Jane said.

"Ah, it sounds like he's one of those daddy doms."

"Daddy doms?" Jane felt her tummy flip and suddenly words she'd heard him utter took on a new meaning. *Good girl. Adorable. Little one. Naughtiness.* Looking up, she saw Sarah smiling. "You really think so? I-I didn't even consider that." She paused, silently thinking that wasn't exactly the truth. Her Kindle was full of books based on a dynamic called ageplay. It had her thinking of all sorts of things, and, to be honest, shuddering quite a bit and not in horror. "Don't you think that's... well, a little weird?"

"Honey, it takes all kinds of people to make up this fascinating thing we call life. If having a daddy dom is what makes your little heart go pitter-patter and dampens your panties, then don't you dare let anyone tell you it's weird or wrong. You're a big girl and only you can really know what makes you feel complete."

"You're a very good friend," Jane said, giving her a hug.

"I love you too," Sarah said, reaching for her book. "Now, don't you have something better to do?"

"Oh!" Jane said, springing up from the couch and dashing back to her bedroom. Jumping onto her bed, she reached for the glass on her nightstand, took a long drink of Coke, and then set it down. "All right, let's see what you want to know."

She smiled when the first screen popped up. It asked about her education and her experiences. She giggled as she wondered what he'd say if she asked him to clarify exactly what *experiences* he was referring to. Then she considered the fact that this screen was asking about her work history, so simply gave the list of jobs she'd held since high school. Pausing, she questioned how he could be interested in her. He obviously had far more education and experience than she had. Taking advantage of the fact that there was a text box at the bottom of the screen, she entered the fact that she'd been saving up to go to culinary school. It wasn't as glamorous as being a philanthropist, but it was her dream. Clicking on the continue button brought up a new screen. These questions asked about her family.

Yes, her parents were still living and, no, she didn't have any siblings. Did she consider herself close to her family? She paused, wondering how to answer. She'd been a 'surprise,' her mother thirty-eight when she'd been born, her father in his mid-forties. While she'd never really felt unwanted, she'd always believed she'd been a bit of an imposition. Still, it wouldn't seem right to say she wasn't close as she figured if push came to shove, she'd be able to rely on some form of support. Clicking the 'yes' box, she continued.

The medical ones were relatively easy as she'd had the chickenpox but not measles, had received the normal vaccines as a child, had never been hospitalized, had no known allergies, and had never broken any bones. She blushed a bit when checking that she'd lost her virginity at seventeen, never had an STD, and, no, while she didn't take the pill, she did practice birth control by receiving a shot every three months. She clicked box after box then hit continue and waited for the next questions to appear.

It wasn't until the fourth screen that she squirmed a bit. These were definitely more invasive but, then again, far better than having to actually look him, or anyone really, in the eye and give her answers. Perhaps this was just a way to cut through all the things one hesitates to discuss? Better to answer in the privacy of her own room, looking at a screen, right? How many sexual partners would be considered too many? One… two? When she realized her fingertip was scrolling the little arrow up and down, she giggled. If there were that many numbers to choose from, she was probably safe with the truth. She'd had three. Okay, that wasn't so hard, was it? No lightning bolt had shot through the ceiling, and no disapproving chorus of 'Jezebel' rang out.

Oh, Lord! Seriously? Did he really need to know these things? How did knowing if she found it easy to reach orgasm help him? *So he can know how long you'll be writhing and begging before gazing into your eyes as you come apart in his arms, of course.*

She considered fibbing a bit about her sexual encounters, suddenly wondering if she was as inexperienced as these questions were making her feel. Far from virginal, she was beginning to feel a bit inadequate. No, she never came from vaginal penetration alone, and she had no idea if anal penetration would get her off as she'd never been brave enough to try that. The very thought made her both squirm and blush furiously. Yes, clitoral stimulation was usually a surety in making her climax. Did she masturbate and, if so, how often? Did she use toys in pleasuring herself? And, shit... did some women really come from nipple stimulation alone? "Lucky ladies," she whispered as she moved to the next screen.

Hard limits. Thanks to her choice of reading materials, she at least knew what most of these were. But how was she supposed to know if they were off-limits if she'd never tried some... okay, almost all of them? Could she even consider that pathetic smack of her last boyfriend's hand against her ass—her denim-covered ass—to be a spanking? It had taken her a lot of courage to ask for Joe to try a little kink, and after only a few strokes, he'd informed her that he felt it ridiculous for a grown woman to want to be spanked. She'd felt humiliated. It had been her first quasi-spanking and their last date. So, she couldn't honestly tick off that she didn't want to at least experience a paddle, a hairbrush, and call her a fool, but her sex had always clenched when reading about the sound of a belt swishing through the air before it landed with a solid thwack on a bare butt. How would she know if the 'line of fire' often described would have her howling and swearing never again, or if it would have her promising to be a good girl? She clicked and unclicked several boxes, changing her answers as she tried to decide what she should enter.

She screamed and practically fell off the bed when suddenly a box appeared superimposed over the list. Oh, God, how could she possibly have forgotten that he was able to see what she was doing?

Jane? Honey, it appears you are having a bit of difficulty. I wanted to assure you that these answers are not chiseled in stone. If you haven't any experience with a question, leave it blank. As we try different implements, positions, and scenarios, you will be able to fill in your answer with honesty. Even then, as you grow and become familiar with various options, what might be a hard limit at first, might change. Remember, there is no judgment, no right or wrong answer. I hope that helps?

It did. She saw a box beneath his and typed: *Yes, sir. It helps—a lot. Thank you.*

You're welcome, little one. If you have any questions, please do not hesitate to ask. I'm here for as long as you need, okay?

She smiled and quickly typed: *Okay.*

Leaving most of the boxes blank, she moved on to the next screen. This section had her heart beating faster. It also had her digging deep. No, she'd not been spanked as a child. Punishment consisted of being sent to her room or grounded. Yes, she sometimes felt overwhelmed. Yes, she thought being held accountable helped a person make better decisions.

After clicking that box, she wondered if she was somehow sealing her fate. Would he consider accountability could only be learned after turning her ass into a burning inferno as his note had stated?

Inferno? Okay, fine, that had been her little addition. Surely he hadn't been completely serious about even the use of the word 'burn'. It was very likely he was using words that painted a picture, allowing them to make his submissive shudder with anticipation. Still, from these questions, it seemed she could expect not to sit comfortably if she disappointed him in some way. With a sigh, she decided to leave the answers she'd given alone. As he'd just said, they weren't chiseled in stone. The last question had her tummy tingling and her mind in a tug of war with her heart.

Have you ever fantasized about having a daddy? She didn't have to wonder what sort of daddy. These questions, this entire website, had nothing to do with biological parenting. This was about roleplaying, fantasy, adults choosing to explore and experience all sorts of sexual kink and erotic play together. But no matter what Sarah had said, if Mr. Masterson was truly a daddy dom, could she be the type of submissive he was looking for? Did she even want to be?

Granted, she didn't own a single piece of sexy-as-sin lingerie, but could she picture herself in some outfit meant to regress her to an age far beneath her chronological one? And God, what if he wanted to treat her as one would an infant? Could she drink from a bottle or wear a diaper? Would he stick a pacifier into her mouth whenever he didn't wish to listen to her? Would she be able to give up her own thoughts, her voice? Finally, with a sigh, she unclicked the 'Yes' box, changing her answer to 'No,' then unclicking it as well.

Her finger hovered over the power button on her laptop and yet she didn't push it. Even though she'd not done it on purpose, she felt she had led him on and now owed him an apology. She began to type in the text box in the lower left corner of her screen.

Daddy…

With a gasp, she pounded the backspace button after realizing what she'd just entered. Taking a deep breath, she began again.

Mr. Masterson—Please don't think that I am judging you or your beliefs, but I feel I must decline your invitation. I do think that you will make some woman very happy… someone waiting to be your special little girl… I just don't think it can be me.

Jane

Sending the text, she didn't wait to see if he would respond, not trusting herself to remain strong and listen to her head and not her heart. This time, she pressed the button to power off her computer and shut the lid. She couldn't help but feel a sense of loss at knowing her journey was over before it began, but she understood the truth. Fantasy was just that… an illusion.

• • • • • • •

Sawyer shook his head as he read Jane's message. His fingers were on the keys, his message halfway completed when he was informed that the connection had been broken—not interrupted, not lost, but terminated. That only happened one way: Jane had shut her computer off. By doing so, she'd not only revoked her permission for him to access her computer remotely, she'd made her choice to terminate any future relationship. He'd lost her.

Shit! No, it was far more likely that this entire process had scared her. That having to sit and look at some faceless computer screen with question after question asking about increasingly more personal details about her life had finally been more than she could take. Hell, it would probably be more than anyone could take. Looking at his screen that only displayed the website logo, he shook his head. It didn't matter that others had been very successful in using technology to find their perfect mate. He knew he'd never again go this route. He also knew that he wasn't ready to give up on Jane. There was something about her that woke every instinct within him. He could already see her in his arms to be cuddled, over his knees to be disciplined, and in his bed to be loved.

He'd seen her eyes, watched her quiver when he'd simply brushed her hair back. Her breath had quickened; her nipples had hardened. The young woman was not disinterested… she was simply too afraid or too embarrassed to admit she had desires she had yet to explore. He had smiled the instant he'd seen the word 'Daddy' appear, expecting her to perhaps ask for more details about the dynamic. But he had watched the five letters disappearing one by one to be replaced by a formal salutation. No, despite her shutting down her computer, he was nowhere near ready to shut off their connection. He'd just go at this a different way. With that decided, he closed his laptop. He wouldn't need it again.

Standing, he left his study. He believed in old-fashioned ways; he'd use that belief to convince Miss Knight that she would indeed be his little one.

CHAPTER FIVE

Sarah plopped down on the couch next to Jane. "Okay, that's enough. You've been moping around all day. I want to know what really happened last night."

Jane sighed. She'd known her friend would have questions but had already said that it just hadn't worked out. "I told you, I got caught up in the fantasy and then reality came crashing down."

"What does that mean?"

"It means I know that I can't be what he is looking for. Sarah, he's not just a dominant, he really is looking for a Little. You know, an adult woman who wants a daddy? Well, that's... that's not me."

"I know what a Little is, and you didn't seem so put off about that possibility last night. In fact, I distinctly remember you being excited about exploring what having a daddy dom would be like."

"Maybe, but what if he makes all sorts of demands that I just can't imagine? What if he wants to put me in diapers or forbids me to speak? Or what if he expects me to crawl around or drink from a bottle? Sleep in some crib all alone? I-I'm just not into that stuff."

Sarah took a moment to respond but then nodded.

"Okay, I can understand that, but you said 'if'. Were those things part of the questions you answered?"

"No, but what else could he be expecting from someone who fantasizes about having a 'daddy'? I just knew that I couldn't be the one he is looking for. I told him I was sorry I wasted his time but, well, didn't wait for his response."

"Wait a minute. He was actually responding… like in real time?"

"Yes, he helped me with a few of the screens, told me not to worry about what I was unsure of, that nothing was written in concrete."

"And yet, with all those reassurances, you didn't bother to ask exactly what he was expecting?"

"Well, no."

Sarah shook her head. "Honey, you didn't terminate the session because you can't be what he wants. You terminated it because you got scared."

"I did not!"

"Say that loud enough and maybe you'll convince yourself," Sarah said, standing and gathering up their coffee mugs before heading toward the kitchen. "You can't possibly deny that there was some sort of instant connection the moment you met. Hell, there were practically sparks shooting between you two. You can't tell me that you weren't beyond excited, that you weren't practically glowing with the anticipation of starting on a journey with this man." She returned with fresh mugs of coffee. Settling on the couch again, she handed one to Jane. "And just by looking at you right now, I know you are wondering if you've made some huge mistake by not taking a chance."

"It doesn't matter. It's over and I'll never see him again," Jane said, standing. "Thanks for the coffee and thanks for caring, but, Sarah, please just let it be, okay?" Ignoring the sympathy in her best friend's eyes, she continued, "I'm going to take a nap. Wake me up in time to get ready for work."

Jane could not believe her eyes. She stood frozen, watching as Sawyer Masterson gave her a smile and a nod as he was escorted to the same table he'd occupied the night before. Despite her terminating the questionnaire, he'd not asked to be seated at any one of the empty tables scattered around the restaurant. No, he'd evidently asked to sit in her section. Instead of approaching, she turned and fled back into the kitchen, running into Sarah, sending the items on the board she'd been holding flying.

"I'm so sorry," Jane said, instantly dropping to pick up the loaf of bread and the small pot of whipped butter.

"You know better than to blast through the… wait, are you okay? You're white as a ghost."

Jane stood, her fingers pressed into the soft dough. "Look, I need you to do me a huge favor. Take table twenty-three."

"Why? Are you ill?" Sarah asked.

"No, well, not exactly," Jane said.

Sarah opened the door a bit and peeked out. "Table twenty-three? So much for not seeing your hunk again."

"He's not mine. I told you, I'm not interested."

Sarah shook her head, a small smile on her lips as she tapped the bread board against her thigh. "You know, if I was into topping, you'd be in so much trouble right now, young lady."

Shocked, Jane just stared at her for a minute, until she asked, "What does that mean?"

"It means that if I was a domme, I'd have you over my lap, and I'd be spanking your little ass for denying what you are desperate to experience."

"Look, I don't want to talk about it. Please, just do this for me without asking any more questions."

Sarah shrugged. "All right, but while I have no problem picturing you as a little princess, I've never really considered you a queen before now."

"Queen?" Jane asked.

"You know, the Queen of De Nile?"

Jane could feel herself blushing as she instantly understood the reference. "I'm not the one in denial, you are if you think I want a daddy. Are you going to help me out or not?"

"Of course. Go take a break before you pass out."

"No, I'm fine now."

"Honey, you've shredded that poor bread and don't even realize it. Take five and get yourself together."

Jane looked down to see nothing but crumbs left in her hands. Dropping the ruined loaf of bread in the trash, she said, "Thanks. I guess I can use a short break."

After spending a few minutes in the break room, reminding herself that she was a grown woman and not some little girl, and immediately feeling her face heat just thinking those words, Jane knew she needed to prove it. She was just about to push through the door when it swung open to reveal Sarah.

"Oh, good, you're looking better," Sarah said. "Look, I'm sorry, but your hunk isn't interested in ordering—"

"So he left? Well, thanks anyway, and stop calling him that!" Jane said, feeling relieved and disappointed.

Sarah shook her head. "You didn't let me finish. He said it was his understanding that he was sitting at one of your tables and would like it if you'd serve him."

"Oh, my God! He actually said he expects me to 'serve' him?"

"Yes. That is what we do here you know? Serve food?" Sarah said and then grinned. "Wait, were you thinking—"

"No! I just..." Jane felt her face flame because serving food had not been the definition that had instantly popped into her head.

"Uh huh, right. Anyway, I told him you were really busy and that I'd be more than happy to wait on him, but he said that he'd prefer to wait until you had a moment."

"But I don't want—"

"Ladies, is there a problem?"

Jane turned to see Mr. Arturo. "Oh, no, sir, no problem."

"Then might I ask you save the chit-chat for after service. We've got a full dining room this evening."

"Of course, sir. I mean, yes, sir. Sorry, sir," Jane said.

As their boss turned away, Sarah grinned and leaned close. "That's a lot of 'sirs'. I'd think you were practicing being a 'good girl'—if, that is, you weren't so adamant about not wanting Mr. Hunk as your daddy dom."

Before Jane could speak, Sarah went back to work while Jane gave herself a little pep talk. She had a job to do and what was that saying? Fake it till you make it? Okay, she could do that. Mr. Masterson had said he'd wait, so... he'd wait.

Plastering a smile on her face, she greeted her other customers, delivered drinks, took food orders, and never stopped moving. Anytime her eyes fell on table twenty-three, she was shocked that he was still sitting there, not showing the least bit of annoyance, giving her a smile before she'd yank her eyes away. Customers at her other tables finished their meals and left, new ones arrived, and still the man remained at the table.

"You know, I don't know what you're trying to prove, but I do know that certain type of men, and I'm positive you know the type I'm referring to, do not find it amusing to be kept waiting," Sarah said the next time Jane went into the kitchen.

"What's he going to do? Spank me?" Jane whispered.

Sarah tilted her head to the side. "Feeling naughty much?"

Whipping her head around, grateful that no one appeared to be listening, Jane spoke even softer. "No, and stop trying to goad me."

"I'm not; I just find it rather interesting that specific consequence was the first one to pop into your head," Sarah assured her. "I was actually thinking more along the lines of what Mr. Arturo must be hearing."

"Mr. Arturo? Why would he... oh, shit," Jane groaned, looking out the window of the door and seeing her boss in conversation with Mr. Masterson. She could only imagine the discussion.

"Good to see you, Sawyer. I've noticed that you've yet to order. Is there a problem?"

"I'm not sure. I'm just waiting for my server, Arnold. You know, that naughty little Jane you hired. She seems to be avoiding my table, but it's only been three hours, so I'm sure she'll be by soon."

Not caring to hear Mr. Arturo's predictable response of how he'd be sure to fire the horrid waitress, Jane grabbed a menu and pushed through the door, searching madly for some type of explanation.

She saw the two men shake hands and when Mr. Arturo turned to leave, his expression gave her no clue as to how upset he had to be. No restaurant owner wanted to see bad service given and that was exactly what she'd done.

"Good evening," she said softly, extending the menu. "I'm sorry—"

"That makes two of us," Sawyer said, cutting her off.

"I don't blame you if you're angry, and I know I'm probably already fired, but please let me make it up to you. Dinner is on me." It would most likely take every penny she'd earned all week in tips and a few additional bucks as well, but she felt just awful.

"That's a very generous offer, but not necessary."

"No, please," Jane gushed. "It's the least I can do." Practically shoving the menu into his hands, she continued, "I'll get you a drink while you decide what you'd like."

Spinning on her heel, she didn't take but a single step when an electrical current stopped her in her tracks. Gasping, she looked down to see his hand on her arm.

"I already know what I want."

"You do? Oh, I mean, that's good. What can I get you?"

"You."

"What?"

"I want you, Jane," he said, his tone causing her to take her eyes off his hand to look up to meet his gaze.

Jane felt her face heating and her heart beating faster. Forget what Sarah had said about them being here to serve liquor and food. Every cell in her body was screaming that what this man wanted was to be served in a very different, very intimate way. "I told you last night that I can't be who you want," she said softly.

"No, you said you didn't *think* you could be," he countered.

"Isn't that the same thing?"

His eyes locked on hers, his fingers lightly stroked across her skin as he said, "Not at all. I'm asking you to allow me to prove it to you, Jane."

Her body began to quiver and yet she shook her head. "I-I can't."

When he smiled and stood, she realized just how tall he was as she had to tilt her head back to look up. And when he pulled her to him, wrapping his arms around her to give her a hug, she had an insane desire to simply melt into his chest.

"Then I shall wait until you can, little one." Before she knew it, he was gone, and she realized that she stood alone in the middle of the restaurant.

CHAPTER SIX

Sawyer saw Jane across the restaurant and his smile of greeting grew wider at the look of disbelief on her face. She'd learn that when he said something, she could count on him being true to his word. Taking the same chair he'd sat in for the last five evenings, he wondered which waitress she'd con into taking over her duties tonight. So far he'd met Sarah, Karen, Megan, Christie, and Gwen. All very attractive young women, but none who drew his interest. No, the only woman he had eyes for was the petite little minx who remained hovering at the door to the kitchen. Jane might be denying that she belonged to him, but Sawyer knew for a fact that she was meant to be his. Every night for almost a solid week, she'd only approached at the end of the evening, and every night he'd assured her that he would wait until she was ready. The moment he saw her shake her head and begin to walk toward him, he knew that tonight would be different.

A glass of water was set down before him. "You know people are starting to talk."

"The only person I'm interested in talking to is you," Sawyer said.

Jane sighed. "The others are wondering if you are some

sort of crazy stalker."

He grinned. "Do you think I'm a stalker, Jane?"

She shook her head and sighed. "No, but I do think you are nuts. Are you seriously going to come in every night and just sit here?"

He picked up his glass and took a sip. "I'm not just sitting here, I'm waiting. And, as I said before, I'll continue to wait until you are ready." He saw the quick smile she was unable to contain and pressed a bit. "But as the man who has committed himself to leading you on the journey you so desperately wish to take, let me say that the longer you wait to take the first step, the longer you will miss out on discovering the happiness waiting for you—for us."

Her smile was delightful but not as much as the widening of her eyes and the pulse he saw quicken in the slim column of her throat.

"You said happiness, but… your message said… alluded that there will be spankings."

"Yes, little one. I'm quite positive that even as wonderful as you are, there will be times when you earn a spanking. But remember, that depends on you."

"I-I thought the dom was always in control," she said, her cheeks flushing.

Reaching up, he tucked a strand of ebony hair behind her ear, his fingertip moving to stroke along her neck, watching her nipples peak to press against the front of her blouse. "That's just one of the many lessons I'm waiting to teach you when you are ready. Be that today, tomorrow, next week, or next year."

"But why? I mean… there are so many women who have experience in… in this. I'm sure they'd love to… to play with you. Why me?"

Did she truly have no idea how special she was? How she'd captured him the first moment she'd asked if she could serve him? He wasn't interested in anyone else. "I'm not asking you to play, Jane. I'm asking you to commit to a relationship that I have absolutely no doubt will be the most incredible one you could imagine."

"And... and if I can't do all you want?"

"That is another lesson you need to learn. There is nothing I would ever do to harm you, nothing I would ever ask that I wasn't sure you want to experience, never take you further than you can go. Just as we spoke about honesty, we discussed trust. Do you remember what I said if you'd give me those two things?"

She nodded and softly said, "You said you'd never abuse either."

He smiled and softly stroked her neck a final time. "And treasure both."

After swallowing hard, Jane said, "All right... you win. I-I'm not promising I can... be what you want, but... but I'd like to try." Before he could speak, she bent forward, her hair swinging like a curtain, partially screening her face as she whispered, "I'm telling you right now, I am not wearing a diaper."

Sawyer smiled and reached up to lay his palm against her cheek. "Good to know you aren't as I don't have one to replace it after I bare your bottom for your spanking." He watched her face color and her eyes widen.

"I-I didn't mean I ever wear... oh... oh, God, I meant—"

"Breathe, little one," Sawyer said, bending forward to place a kiss on her forehead. "I know what you mean, and now I'm pretty sure I know why some little girl got scared and shut down her computer." Her look of guilt told him he was correct. "And knowing that you've most likely spent many hours worrying about things unnecessarily, I believe it is time for us to take that first step. Shall we?"

"What? Now?" she asked, followed quickly by, "I-I can't. I have to work."

Sawyer chuckled. "One of the perks of being good friends with your boss is that I'm quite positive he will understand. And, young lady, I'm not about to let you out of my sight until we finish that discussion we began, and I don't think you want to have it in the middle of a busy restaurant."

Her face turned a darker shade of pink and her teeth captured her bottom lip. He stood and extended his hand, smiling when she slipped hers into it. "Let's go tell Sarah that I'll be taking you home."

"Okay," she said softly.

He couldn't wait until she added 'Daddy' to her responses, but for now, just having her hand in his was worth every moment he'd spent waiting. Once in the kitchen, he smiled as Arnold approached with a large bag.

"Thank you," Sawyer said, accepting it.

"You're welcome, and, Miss Knight, I don't expect to see you for at least two weeks. Understand?"

"But I'm scheduled to work—"

"I've adjusted the schedule," Arnold said with a smile. "You're an exemplary employee but there are some things that are more important than work. Take the time to discover that for yourself."

"Thank you," she said.

Sarah stepped forward and Sawyer released Jane's hand so the two women could hug. "I'm so glad you finally saw the light," Sarah said with a smile. "Oh, and I'm going out after work, so don't wait up for me."

"And thanks," Karen said with a huge grin. "Another half-hour and I would have lost, but thanks to you, I can finally get those Jimmy Choos I've been coveting."

"What? You-you all bet on me?"

"No, we actually bet on Mr. Masterson," Sarah clarified. "We all knew it was just a matter of time before you realized that any man willing to sit and wait was worth getting to know."

Sawyer chuckled and Jane just shook her head in disbelief. After getting her purse from the break room, he took her hand again, leading her out of the restaurant. Her eyes grew wide again when a silver sedan pulled up, the driver exiting the vehicle to come around to the side.

"Jane, I'd like you to meet Richard. Richard, this is Miss Jane Knight."

"It's a pleasure to meet you, miss," Richard said, giving a brief nod of his head as he opened the back door.

"Hello," Jane said, looking from him to Sawyer. "You have a driver?"

"Sometimes I do," Sawyer said. "Tonight I'd prefer spending my time focusing on you rather than on the roads." He slipped his hand to the small of her back and guided her into the car, sliding in beside her.

Once he closed the door, Richard slid behind the wheel. Sawyer gave him an address after which the divider between the front and back raised.

"How did you know my address?" Jane asked. Before he could answer, she smiled. "Never mind, I forgot you're some sort of computer nerd."

"Nerd?"

She giggled and he found the sound delightful. "I didn't mean it in an insulting way. I just meant you could access my computer…"

When she abruptly stopped speaking, he took her hand. "That was only with your permission. The moment you terminated the session, that permission was revoked. I will never invade your privacy, Jane."

"Oh, okay." After a moment, she said, "May I ask you a question?"

"I'm sure you'll be asking many questions, and I will always answer if I am able to do so, or explain why I can't."

Her voice dropped to a mere whisper as her eyes darted toward the front seat. "Can Richard hear us?"

"Not unless I press the intercom button. But let me assure you that if he could, you'd need not worry. He is very discreet and would never divulge anything he might witness."

She looked up at him. "You're not just a dom, are you? I mean, you are more of a daddy dom?"

"I am many things, but, yes, I would consider it a great

honor if you'd allow me to be your daddy as well."

"What... what if I don't like it? I mean, you sounded very determined about the... the spanking part?"

Sawyer smiled and had her seatbelt unbuckled and pulled her onto his lap before she could protest. Wrapping his arms around her, he bent to kiss her cheek. "You're correct in that I'm a determined man in many aspects. And, baby girl, the truth is that if you like it, then I won't be doing it right. A punishment spanking is just that—punishment. It is supposed to hurt. It is intended to teach you the consequences of misbehavior in hopes that you learn not to repeat the misdeed. If your little bottom isn't burning by the time I let you off my lap or release you from a position you've taken to receive discipline, then what would be the point?"

"We could just discuss any... um—"

"Naughtiness?" he offered with a grin. "We could and we shall. I will make sure that you know exactly why you are going to be spanked, but it is my responsibility as your daddy to not only take care of you, but to help you become the best person you can be. If, as you say, you don't like being spanked, then remember what I said about control. Control your behavior and you will control your need to be disciplined."

She sighed, not speaking for several minutes and then looked up at him. "You said 'punishment spanking' like there is some other kind."

"There is," Sawyer said, giving her a little hug. "And those kinds of spankings are ones I promise you will enjoy."

It was obvious she doubted him by the way her forehead furrowed, but then she smiled. "I think I've read about those kinds. Funishment—that's the name, right?"

"Yes, that's one term, but I like to think of them as 'good girl spankings'."

"Maybe we should start with one of those," she suggested, causing him to chuckle and hold her tighter.

"Good try, but not tonight."

"Why not? I thought I was in control. That I got to decide."

Taking her chin in his fingers, he tilted her head so that their eyes locked. "You did decide the moment you took that first step. Tell me, do you honestly feel that you haven't been the least bit naughty? That you don't feel a little guilty about the way you've behaved not only toward me, but toward your coworkers and Mr. Arturo?"

"I-I guess."

"You guess?"

Her shifting on his lap answered the question before she nodded. He bent forward and kissed her forehead. "I'll let you in on a little secret. I know you're a little scared, but, I promise, the moment the spanking is over, you'll feel much better."

She sighed, but when she laid her head against his chest, her body relaxing into him, he smiled and treasured the trust she was gifting him with.

CHAPTER SEVEN

Jane was very glad that she'd been so determined to keep her mind off of Sawyer that she'd cleaned the entire house. Passing him the key when he held out his hand, she waited until he opened the door, loving the feel of his hand against her back as he stepped aside to allow her to enter first. It wasn't until the door closed that she wondered how that same hand would feel against a different part of her anatomy.

"Relax, little one."

"What?"

"You're trembling. You have nothing to worry about."

She couldn't help herself, rolling her eyes and shaking her head. "Easy for you to say. You're going to be the one doing the smacking."

When he chuckled, she couldn't believe she heard herself asking, "So, where do you want me?"

"At the table," Sawyer said.

Her eyes flicked to the table, imagining herself bent across its top, her hands gripping the edge as he pushed up her skirt and… She gave a little squeal as he touched her. Not to lift her clothing, but to slip an arm around her waist as he smiled and held up the bag that Arnold had given him.

"We'll eat first."

She could feel her face heat. "Oh... um, okay. I'll set the table."

"No, you just sit down," Sawyer countered, placing the bag on the table and pulling a chair out for her.

"Why? You don't know where anything is."

He shook his head. "Because Daddy said he wants you to sit down. I can see that you're still wincing a bit. I want you off your feet." He guided her to take a seat and then squatted, lifting her foot and removing her shoe. "Your ankle is still a bit swollen from the other night." He removed her other shoe and then gently massaged both ankles. "We'll have that checked out during your doctor's appointment."

"I'm sure it's fine," she protested.

His eyebrow quirked as he looked up at her, his fingers still palpating the ankle she'd twisted the first night they'd met. "I see we are going to have to clear up a few things. The first being that when your daddy says you'll be having your ankle checked, then, baby girl, you will be having it examined."

She could only nod.

After a final, gentle rub, he stood and bent to kiss her cheek. "Now, direct me to the dishes and we'll eat."

Jane watched as he fixed her plate, cut her steak into bite-sized pieces, dabbed butter and sour cream on her baked potato, added a spoonful of broccoli and then set it in front of her. Only then did he serve himself.

Suddenly she remembered what he'd said. "You said at my doctor's appointment but I don't have an appointment."

"You will," Sawyer said. "The sooner we get the necessary details attended to, the sooner we can play."

Though she wanted to ask what he meant about 'playing', she lost her nerve. Instead, she asked, "What necessary details?"

"You'll need a physical and—"

"Why? I mean, I told the truth on the questions. I'm really a healthy person. I haven't been sick in ages and—"

"And you were just naughty. Can you tell me what you just did?"

Naughty? Jane was taken aback. All she'd been doing was trying to explain that she didn't want a physical. "Um... I disagreed with you?"

"No, sweetie, you interrupted me when I was speaking. That isn't only impolite, it is disrespectful."

"I was just... you're right. I'm sorry."

"Good girl. Admitting you made a mistake is a good thing and apologizing for that mistake is another. As I was saying, you *will* have a physical as I need to be certain that you are not only healthy, but physically able to tolerate certain things."

"Tolerate what? Like can I tolerate a spanking?"

He chuckled and shook his head. "No, I'm positive that while you might not like a spanking, you'll certainly be able to tolerate one. I'm talking about other things."

Jane played with her food more than she ate it, but she couldn't help it. Forget 'other things', all she could think about was the spanking he'd promised. Finally, she set her fork down. "I'm not trying to be difficult, but I really don't think I can eat. Not when I'm so nervous."

Reaching across the table, he covered her hand with his. "Being a bit nervous is normal, but I don't want you to be so unsettled that it interferes with your ability to eat. Dinner can wait a bit."

"Thank you." His grin had her thinking she must sound foolish as she'd basically just thanked him in advance for the spanking he was about to deliver. "I didn't mean for the..."

"Jane, relax. I know what you mean." He stood and helped her from her chair. With her hand in his, he looked down. "Do you need to go to the bathroom first?"

"The bathroom. Why?"

"Because I don't want you to be uncomfortable."

Jane almost giggled thinking how could he expect her to be comfortable getting her butt smacked. Fortunately, she managed to keep a straight face. "Okay, I'll be right back."

She hurried out of the room, suddenly grateful to have an excuse to be alone if only for a few minutes. Once inside the bathroom, she relieved herself and then stood in front of the mirror as she washed her hands. "You need to get a grip, Jane," she said softly. "You wanted this, remember? It's not like you're going to your execution—it's just a little spanking, right?" Nodding at her reflection, she dried her hands, ran a brush through her hair, and then took a deep breath and opened the door.

Despite giving herself a pep talk, the moment she entered the living room and saw the chair he'd brought in from the dining room, her tummy flipped. When he smiled and held out his hand, she went to him on shaky legs, allowing him to guide her between his legs. She was pretty sure that if he let her go, she'd fall straight to the floor, and she was grateful that his hands continued to hold both of hers, not letting her collapse at his feet.

"Tell me why Daddy is going to spank his little girl."

Whoa, this was really happening! The question, the terms of address, the tone, everything about it seemed surreal and yet she found herself answering, "Because I-I was bad?"

"Not bad, Janie, naughty. How were you naughty?"

She didn't really understand the difference, but what she did understand was that he—her daddy—had just given her a Little name. How a simple thing could have such a profound effect on her, she didn't know, but it did. Instantly she felt years fall away and that allowed her to answer.

"I was rude to you, took advantage of my friends, and wasn't a very good employee."

"And you lied."

"I didn't!"

"Yes, sweetie, you did. You've been lying since the first night when you refused to acknowledge that this is exactly what you've been wanting, craving, for so very long. Now, how does that make you feel inside?"

How could he sound so sure of himself? Of her. She'd

not even completed the section about having a daddy. It was as if he didn't require her written answers, just needed to look at her and know this was what she had been searching for. "Not very good," she admitted and recognized the truth of that statement. "A little icky actually."

"That's what guilt does, but Daddy is going to make that icky feeling go away." Releasing her hands, he guided them to her sides. "How is Daddy going to do that, Janie?"

"You're going to spank me."

"That's right. In the future, I might ask you to drop your panties, lift your skirt, and place yourself over my knee or position yourself elsewhere, but since this is your first spanking, I'm going to help, all right?"

"All... all right." Her breath caught in her throat when his hands slipped beneath her skirt and her knees started shaking even more when he hooked his fingers in the waistband of her panties. She wasn't sure exactly how she'd pictured this happening, but it hadn't been this. It was as if his body temperature was transferring to her skin with every tug of her underwear as he began to lower them. Her face flamed and her tummy began doing somersaults. She couldn't for the life of her hold back the small whimper when the thin fabric conquered the hillocks of her buttocks, leaving them bare. He didn't release them until they were at her knees, just visible beneath the hem of her skirt. With a simple movement, he turned her slightly and she gave a short yip of surprise when he tipped her over his left leg.

"Brace your hands on the floor," he instructed. "I've got you. You won't fall."

Planting her palms on the floor, she was grateful that her hair cascaded around her face, her gratitude for the coverage growing exponentially when she felt her skirt being lifted and folded back to expose her bottom.

"Do not reach back, Janie. Keep your hands and feet down."

"O-okay."

"That's my good girl."

His words, the feel of his hand laying across her ass, and the feel of his free arm hugging her just a little closer to his body made Jane feel secure, but the moment she felt his right leg lifting to capture both of hers, she started to panic.

"Wait! Is-is this going to hurt?"

"Yes, it is."

Why those three little words didn't have her fighting like a wildcat to get free, she'd never understand. Perhaps it was that he didn't sugarcoat it, didn't lie, didn't even assure her that it wouldn't be *that* bad, but whatever the reason, they managed to settle her in the mindset of a little girl who'd chosen to misbehave and who had a daddy who wouldn't allow her to be naughty without consequence. But when she felt his hand disappear, she knew that she'd earned this spanking and was finally ready to accept her just deserts.

The first strike shocked her enough that she remained absolutely silent, the second had her drawing in a huge gulp of air, the third had her head rearing back, and the fourth had her finding her voice as she shrieked. Hell, yes, it hurt! This was nothing like the time she'd been over Joe's knees for that ridiculous facsimile of a spanking. Sawyer's hand, the same hand that had made her feel so small, so secure as he'd held hers, was now falling like a paddle. It was hard and it was huge enough to cover a great deal of territory with each swat.

"Ow, ow, ow! Please!"

He ignored her cries, the sound of each crack of his hand bouncing about the room as she was sure her butt was bouncing beneath each stroke. No longer worried about the embarrassment of her position, no longer caring that he was staring at her bare bottom, all Jane was concerned about was surviving the spanking.

"Please! I'm sorry! I'll never be naughty again, I swear!"

"Settle down, Janie. We've only just started and promises made while getting a spanking are rarely kept."

Another half dozen strokes and she was sure she'd never sit again. Jane wanted to curse the lack of carpeting as her fingers clawed at the floor, her nails scraping over useless hardwood that didn't allow a grip. Trying to kick her feet was thwarted by his leg pinning hers. Still, she couldn't remain still. She wiggled, she squirmed, and she attempted to buck like a bronco with a burr under its saddle. When all that failed, she whipped her hands back, waving them in the air, attempting to block even a single swat.

"Naughty," he said, capturing both of Jane's wrists, pinning them against the small of her back. "Little girls who misbehave during their spanking earn extra strokes."

"No! Please, I didn't mean to! Please, that's enough!"

"Daddy decides what is enough. Not you, Janie." With that, his knee lifted, her face lowered and she discovered that her bottom was not the only place that her daddy could turn into a furnace. When he began to swat the area where her bottom merged with her thighs, Jane gasped and then burst into tears.

"I'm sorry, Daddy! I'm sorry!" The fact that she'd just called him Daddy for the first time registered and yet it didn't seem strange or forced... it felt just right.

"I know you are, baby girl, but it's my job to make sure you understand that naughtiness will earn you a hot little bottom every time."

Evidently her new daddy took his job very seriously because his hand kept rising and falling. Jane was soon nothing more than a blubbering blob, limp over his knee, strands of her hair stuck to her cheeks, her poor butt feeling as if an entire continent of killer bees had decided to sink their stingers into her flesh. She had no idea when the spanking ended, only that instead of another stroke, she felt his hand rubbing gently over her throbbing buttocks.

"Shhh, it's over now." Before she could react, Sawyer released her wrists and lifted her, flipping her over and cradling her against his chest, her bottom resting on his thigh. Jane grabbed onto his shirt, burying her face in his neck and just wailed.

"That's it, little one. Let it all out. You're safe. Daddy's got you."

She didn't even question the validity of that statement. No matter how much she'd struggled and squirmed, he'd never once allowed her to feel as if she'd tumble to the floor. This position might be different, but she knew that he'd keep her close, hold her tight until she was ready to pull away. Why she didn't immediately jump off his lap, order him out of her house, and inform him that she never wanted to set eyes on him again was a question for another time. Right now, all she wanted was to feel his arms around her, his hand stroking her back, and the feel of his solid chest against her body.

Minutes passed as Jane calmed and went from thinking about how much her bottom hurt to thinking about how wonderful it felt to be in his arms. Finally, she gave a last sniffle and sat back. Immediately, he had a handkerchief ready and gently wiped her face and then softly instructed her to blow. Once that was done, he gave her a smile and a kiss that had her insides beginning to burn. The kiss was gentle and yet so full of promise that she found it a little difficult to breathe. When he pulled away, she instantly wanted his lips to return to hers.

"Better?"

"Yes," she managed. "You were right, you know."

"About what?"

"Spankings really do hurt!"

He chuckled and gave her a hug. "Then I did my job correctly. Just know that the next time you lie, either to me or yourself, you'll bend over for my belt."

Who knew that hearts could actually stop mid-beat and that his words would have her freshly spanked butt clenching and another rush of moisture slipping into the folds of her sex? She couldn't help but look at his waist, the belt threaded through its loops seeming to give weight to his words. Her hand dropped from where it had been clutching his shirt and reached down, a finger moving toward the black leather. Before she could touch it, she became aware of the fact that the front of his trousers looked very... full and she could swear she saw something—okay, his cock—twitch beneath the fabric. Yanking her hand away, she snapped her eyes back to his, seeing a slight curve to his lips and his eyebrow arched. She was pretty sure she wasn't supposed to be thinking about his cock when he was discussing her punishment. Nodding, she hoped that he'd think she'd simply been listening to him.

"O-okay."

He gave her a little squeeze. "Other than your bottom being a little tender, how do you feel here?" His finger tapped against her chest, right over her heart.

Jane considered the question and gave him the only answer she could. "Guilt-free and... and really good."

"That's the benefit of a spanking. You pay for your transgression and all is forgiven. You have a clean slate." When her stomach rumbled, he grinned. "And now that you're no longer nervous, you can enjoy dinner." Lifting her off his lap, it took her a second to realize why he was bending forward. Seeing him reach for her panties that were now at her ankles, she felt her face heat, her head knocking into his as she also bent, ready to take them from him.

"Are you all right?" he asked, his eyes lifting to hers.

Dropping her hand where she'd been rubbing her forehead, she said, "Yes, sorry, I just... I can do that."

"I know," he acknowledged, and yet didn't even hesitate to continue pulling her panties up her legs before bending forward to kiss her forehead. "But, that's also part of my job."

There wasn't really enough time to be embarrassed as the cotton undies were already covering her punished nates before she could blink. Once her panties were back where they belonged, he patted her bottom gently and then stood, taking her hand in one of his while the other easily lifted the chair.

Jane discovered that while she'd been in the bathroom,

DADDY SAYS

he'd put their plates in the oven to keep their dinners warm. After he placed the chair back where it belonged, she eyed the wooden seat and decided that cushions were a definite addition to her shopping list. She was trying to determine how to ask if she could remain standing, when he set her plate down, not where it had been originally, but next to his.

"Come here," he said, taking a seat and patting his knee.

Climbing into his lap was far more comfortable than any cushion and taking bites from the fork he offered to her lips felt as natural as feeding herself. As they ate, she settled against his chest, feeling a sense of peace she'd never experienced before. He wasn't making her feel strange about the spanking or looking at her like she was some sort of weirdo for needing him to be in control. She didn't understand it exactly, but did she really need to?

After they both finished eating, she hopped from his lap and began to gather the dishes, surprised when he helped her clean the kitchen. It took no time at all with the two of them working together. "Do you want some coffee?" she asked.

"No, not tonight. You need to get into bed."

"Bed? It's early still. I thought maybe we could watch a movie or something."

Sawyer hung the dish cloth on the rack and shook his head. "I'd love to, but not tonight. You've got an early doctor's appointment tomorrow and need to get your rest."

"Tomorrow? But I haven't even made an appointment yet. We don't need to rush into this."

He tilted his head to the side, giving her a long look. "Are you scared of doctors, Janie?"

Remembering how he felt about lying, she put her hand behind her back and crossed her fingers. "Of course not."

"Hmm, well, from what you just said, I have a feeling that it's been quite some time since you've seen a doctor, correct?"

"So? I've told you I'm healthy," Jane said, not about to tell him she hadn't gone to a doctor since she'd been a teen and had mono.

Sawyer shook his head. "Regular appointments are necessary to make sure you remain healthy. But, no worries as I called and made the appointment when you were in the bathroom. I'll be by at eight in the morning."

"But—"

He took her hand and pulled her to him. "No arguments, and remember, I'll be with you every step of the way. Now, if you'd like, I'll tuck you into bed before I leave."

The jump from doctor's visits to being tucked in was a little startling, but she eagerly made the transition. "I'd like that."

"All right. Run and change into your jammies, and I'll be in."

Nodding, she went to her room trying to figure out how she could tell him that what she'd really like was for him to tuck himself into her bed as well. As she changed into a pink nightgown that had an edging of lace around the hem and bodice, she realized she wasn't even sure that he was interested in any sort of adult relationship. She'd answered questions about her likes and dislikes, but those had come before the section on ageplay. Was she even on the same page as Sawyer?

"You ready?"

The question had her twirling around, her heart pounding a bit.

"Sorry, I didn't mean to scare you."

"No, you just surprised me," she said, sure her face was as red as her butt, but suddenly positive that she could not suggest he climb in beside her.

He smiled and looked around her room. "Which stuffy would you like?"

"Oh, um, I really don't sleep with those," Jane said, a bit mortified that she hadn't even considered that he might be in her bedroom one day. She was pretty sure that grown women did not normally keep, much less display, an entire shelf of beloved stuffies from their childhood.

"No? That seems like a shame," he said, turning his eyes back to her.

Jane busied herself yanking back the quilt and sheet on the bed, hopping in and biting back the moan that threatened to escape as her bottom took her full weight. Sawyer came to the side and sat down on the edge of the bed, tucking the covers around her. Leaning down, he kissed the tip of her nose.

"Are we going to have sex?" The moment she realized she'd just blurted that out, she almost died of embarrassment.

He sat back and shook his head. "No—"

Of course they weren't. He wasn't just a dom, he was a daddy dom. "Never mind; it was a stupid question. I mean, it's clear you want a daddy/little relationship. Just forget I asked. You-you can go now."

"No," he repeated, smiling down at her. "I most certainly will not go. Not until we get a few things straight. You worried yourself sick for a week thinking that I'd have you in diapers and drinking out of a bottle instead of just asking, so, honey, know that there are no stupid questions." As he spoke, he kicked off his shoes and pulled away the covers he'd just tucked in. "Scooch over." He moved to sit with his back against the headboard, and when he reached for her, she didn't hesitate to climb onto his lap. "All right, baby girl, let's talk."

CHAPTER EIGHT

Having her in his arms felt as perfect as he'd imagined. But, it was clear that she was still confused and that wouldn't do. It was imperative that she understand exactly what he desired—what he knew she would find equally fulfilling.

"Janie, I'm not just your daddy, but I'm also a man. You are a woman who also needs to be a Little at times. There are infinite definitions of how couples define their relationships, how they see their roles, but unless you tell me otherwise, as far as I'm concerned—yes, there will be sex. A lot of sex."

"There will?" she asked, her cheeks turning scarlet but her eyes going brighter. "I just didn't want to… to assume that you're, well, attracted to me in that way."

"Baby, believe me, I'm very attracted to you, and I know that you're quite attracted to me as well."

"How? We haven't really done much other than kissing and that was nice… but it was the kind of sweet and innocent sort of kissing."

"True, and while spanking isn't exactly fun for you, it does tell me quite a bit about your responses." Seeing the doubt in her eyes, he smiled. "Even though you were nervous about being spanked, your body tells its own story.

When I pulled down your panties, they were damp. Every time you kicked your feet or wiggled your bottom, I could see that your little pussy was glistening." When she groaned and buried her face in his shirt, he cupped her chin and made sure she was looking into his eyes. "That is nothing to be embarrassed about or feel ashamed of. Spanking is a very intimate thing. I'm not only touching your bare skin, I'm watching your responses, and, Janie, what I saw made me very pleased."

"You liked spanking me?"

"Not liked in the way you mean, but, yes. I liked the fact that you trusted me to do so, to give you a bit of pain in order to help you become the person you want to be. I don't like hearing you cry, but do like knowing that once the spanking is over, you'll feel better, forgiven. Punishing you is but one of my responsibilities. Pleasuring you will be another."

"Like when you give me a funishment spanking?"

He grinned, his cock rock hard as he visualized her perfect ass up in the air, her sharp yips of pain at each stroke turning to moans of pleasure as he soothed away the sting. "Yes, like that or when I lay you down and kiss you in a far less sweet and innocent way, nibbling on your nipples and licking the cream from your pussy."

"You... you could do that now," she said.

"I know, but I don't believe in pleasuring after a punishment. Not to say that I won't take my own pleasure at times when you've been naughty, and even use your body hard as part of an intimate punishment, but as far as immediately bringing you to orgasm, I believe that negates the lesson. Can you understand that?"

She took a moment, her eyes wide before she shook her head. "I'm not sure as I'm still wondering about who exactly is in control here. You said I was but from what you're saying, you are free to get your rocks off while I'll be left with nothing but a burning butt."

"You are in control of yourself, your choices so to speak.

If you make the wrong ones, you'll be punished, which is what I am in control of. If you don't want to have a burning bottom at the very least, then be my good girl. It's really as simple as that."

He'd said there were no stupid questions and was glad when she didn't hesitate to ask another. "What do you mean, the very least?"

"There are many places where a naughty girl can be spanked." Tilting her forward just a bit, he reached to give her bottom a squeeze. "Your ass." Sliding his hand beneath her gown, his fingers trailed along the curve of her bottom cheeks. "This sweet little area called your sit-spot, which you experienced tonight." Dropping his hand an inch, he stroked her thigh. "The backs of your thighs." Moving his hand, he heard her gasp as he stroked a finger against the gusset of her panties. "Your little pussy when you are exceptionally naughty can also receive a spanking." Her bottom lip was between her teeth as he continued his demonstration by moving higher and cupping her breast. "And your breasts."

"You'd spank my breasts?"

"Yes, I would. I will never lie to you, Janie. There is not a single part of your body that won't belong to me. I'll spank you whenever and wherever I deem is necessary, and you will know you are being punished." His fingers moved to gently stroke across her nipple, the bud already puckered tightly. "I will also lick, suckle, kiss, taste every inch of your skin to bring you pleasures you've yet to imagine. There will be no inch of you that I will leave unexplored. You'll take my cock into your mouth and your cunny for both pleasure and penance. And, Janie, you'll take every single inch of my cock into your tight little ass when I am making love to you or if I'm giving you a hard punishment fuck."

Her breathing was becoming ragged as he spoke, her nipples hard as stones, her eyes a bit glazed and yet she didn't attempt to pull away, didn't voice a single objection.

"Is there any part of that you don't want, Janie?"

"N-no, sir."

His instincts had just been validated. She'd not enjoy it all, but she craved it, and he would make it his life's work to make sure she realized what an incredible gift her submission to him was.

"Good girl. Just trust me, sweetie. Trust me as your daddy, as your lover, as the man who wants to be your everything."

"I... I'll try."

Bending, he took her mouth. Not softly as he'd done after her spanking, but hard. She instantly pressed against him, her arms wrapping around his neck, her body trembling as he stroked his tongue against the seam of her lips, demanding entrance. She opened and he invaded, plundered, took her breath away as she clung to him. His cock throbbed, and he had no doubt that if he laid her back, if he spread her legs, she'd welcome him inside her pussy. But he would not take her tonight. He released her, then kissed her softly before pulling away completely, loving her soft mewl of protest.

"And that is why you will see the doctor tomorrow. There will be no sex until I'm positive that you are healthy—"

"How many times do I have to say, I am healthy?"

She squealed when he took her nipple between his thumb and finger and pinched. "That's twice now you've interrupted Daddy."

"I'm sorry!"

Releasing the puckered bud, he said, "I was also going to say it is important that I know your capabilities." When her mouth opened, he placed a finger against her lips. "Trust me, Janie." She nodded and he gave her a quick kiss. Sometimes it wasn't easy being in control—not when it required restraint, but that was also part of his responsibility.

"Does that answer your question at least for a start?"

"Yes," she said, her voice soft, her eyes even softer.

Sawyer smiled, lifted her into his arms only long enough

to stand and then slipped her back between the sheets. Tucking the blankets around her again, he bent to kiss her one last time. "Get some sleep."

"I will and, um, Daddy?"

"Yes?"

"Do you... spank for a sort of fib?"

"How do you 'sort of fib'?"

She glanced at the shelf he'd looked at earlier. "I don't sleep with those, but I do sleep with Mr. Bear."

He grinned, actually quite pleased that she trusted him enough to risk a spanking to admit she enjoyed a stuffy. "And where is he?"

"Over on the chair."

The bear did indeed look like he was used to being cuddled. After retrieving him, he tucked the stuffy beneath the covers next to her. Dropping a kiss on her lips, he stood and looked down at her. "Since I don't have a 'sort of spanking', I'm going to let that little fib go." She grinned and he shook his head. "Only this one time, young lady. Do not fib to me again because you already know what will happen."

Her eyes locked once more on the belt around his waist, and she shuddered. "I won't, Daddy."

"All right. Goodnight, Janie."

"Goodnight, Daddy."

Sawyer flicked off the light and walked back through the house. It wasn't until he had the front door open that he thought about one last instruction, and something was telling him it was an important one. Closing the door softly, he retraced his steps. He'd left her bedroom door slightly ajar and he pushed it open. Sure enough, his intuition had been spot-on. Janie was not curled on her side with Mr. Bear in her arms. In fact, she wasn't even tucked in tightly. His little one had the covers down at her waist and from the soft sounds he could hear and the movement he could discern, he had a very good idea of exactly what she was doing. Two steps took him to the side of her bed, and a single tug of the blankets had her screeching and her eyes flying open.

"Young lady, what are you doing?"

"God, you scared me!" she said, as he flipped the light on.

It took everything within him not to grin as she didn't move a muscle, thinking perhaps that if she remained frozen he couldn't figure out exactly where her hand was. "Pull it out, little one."

Her hand slowly emerged from her underwear, her fingers curling into a fist. He reached down and took her hand, opening her fist to reveal the wetness coating her fingers.

"You are not allowed to masturbate. From now on, all your orgasms belong to me. Daddy will be the one to decide when his little one receives pleasure. Is that clear?"

"Always?"

"Yes, sweetie. The moment you agreed to give yourself to me, to honor me by becoming my special girl, every little inch of you became mine. Understand?"

"I-I didn't know."

"That is why your panties aren't already down and your bottom up."

He could practically see her mind spinning, knew her need, could smell her arousal and yet she needed to understand that this was the beginning of her total immersion into her submission. "Did you hear me, Janie?"

It took her a moment to say, "Yes, Daddy."

"Good girl. And if you think about disobeying once I leave, if you are a naughty girl and allow your fingers to play where they don't belong, I promise that you'll regret it."

"Why... I mean... it's not like I've never... or that you'll kn..." He watched as a wave of color ran up from the neck of her gown to stain her face as she stumbled over her words.

Sawyer shook his head as she admitted that masturbation wasn't a foreign concept and basically told him that she wasn't worried about his finding out she'd ignored his instruction. Neither one of those was conducive to building a relationship... especially one as intimate and based on a level of deep trust as the dynamic of daddy/little, which was exactly what they both wanted.

"Because while you will experience a few moments of pleasure, instead of sweet dreams, you'll find your mind will be filled with visions of you squirming and thinking about how you were naughty, how you disobeyed your daddy's wishes. Unless you want to toss and turn picturing yourself making your confession, placing yourself over my knee and presenting your little bottom for a much longer, much harder spanking than the one you received earlier, including several swats on your little pussy, I'd suggest you consider if a few seconds of bliss is worth it." He paused as if knowing she needed a moment to collect herself and then he said, "And, Janie?"

"Yes, sir?"

"I assure you I *will* know." He heard her gasp as he drew each of her fingers into his mouth and licked away the evidence of her naughtiness. Once her hand was clean, he tucked the covers back around her, making sure Mr. Bear was in her arms this time. "Goodnight, my sweet girl."

"Good... goodnight, Daddy."

CHAPTER NINE

Despite waking up hours before she normally would have, Jane knew she was running out of time. She'd already changed clothes a half-dozen times. What did one wear when spending their first full day together? "Definitely not this ratty shirt," she mumbled, yanking it off. She'd just pulled on a button-down, sleeveless blouse in a soft yellow hue when the doorbell rang. Shocked that it could already be eight, she tugged on a skirt and then ran to the door even as she pushed small buttons through their corresponding holes. She didn't want the bell to wake Sarah.

"Good morning, Janie," Sawyer said, smiling down at her.

She'd already known he was very handsome, but today, dressed more casually in a pair of gray trousers and a white button-down shirt, instead of a suit, he seemed even more so. His black hair made his blue eyes appear even more vivid. "Good morning, Daddy."

"May I come in?"

"Oh, yes, of course. I just need to run and get my shoes…" Her words cut off when, after stepping into the house, his hands reached out.

"Let me help you, honey."

She felt her tummy flip when his fingers brushed the front of her blouse, and as the first button was pushed free, she lost her breath.

"Some little girl was in a hurry dressing, wasn't she? You've misbuttoned your blouse."

As he quickly and efficiently freed each button, she could feel her face heat. He wasn't about to caress her... he was dressing her properly. Before she could worry about what he'd think seeing that her bra was doing a very poor job of concealing nipples that had hardened the moment he'd reached for her, he was done. And before she could feel too terribly disappointed, he pulled her to him, giving her a hug and bending to give her a kiss. It was a soft meeting of lips, but it heated her blood.

Lifting his head, he smiled again. "I've been waiting to do that again ever since I left you last night."

"Me too," she admitted softly.

"Run and get your shoes and a sweater. I don't want you to get chilled."

She nodded and was soon back, her white sandals on her feet and a sweater over her arm. "I didn't know what to wear," she confessed.

"You chose well. You look fresh as a daisy," he said, taking the sweater from her and helping her into it. "Ready to go?"

Sliding her cell phone into her purse, she slipped the strap over her shoulder. "I guess, but I could really use a cup of coffee."

"We'll get something to eat in just a little bit," he assured her. He placed a hand at the small of her back and led her from the house. After she'd closed the door, he jiggled the knob to assure it was locked and then reached down and took her hand.

"Where's Richard?"

"I do like to drive occasionally," he said, settling her into the front seat, reaching across to buckle her in, then pressing a kiss to her forehead before shutting her door and moving around the car.

Once he was seated, she angled her body toward him. "I have a confession to make."

He looked over, his eyebrow quirked and she felt her face flush, his words of the evening before replaying in her head.

"Not about that… I mean, I didn't, you know…"

"Play without permission?"

"Um, yes. I mean, no, I didn't…"

He chuckled and reached over to give her hand a squeeze. "Breathe, sweetie, and just tell me."

"I googled you that first night," she blurted out.

"Good girl."

"You're not mad?"

"Of course not. I'm actually pleased. It's very important to be safe in this world, and the fact that you did a bit of research before making such a serious commitment tells me you are cautious."

"May I ask you something?"

He looked over at her as they'd pulled to a stop at a light. "Remember, I've said that you may always ask me anything. This is new to you. I'd be very surprised if you don't have about a million questions going through your head."

She'd not really been thinking about that, but his words had her asking her first question. "But not new to you?"

"Just like you, I've had other relationships before," he said, giving her hand another squeeze before returning his hand to the wheel. "But you are the only young woman I've seen as favored, and the only one who is important to me now."

"But you've had a Little before?"

He looked at her again and smiled. "Janie, I'm not a man to kiss and tell, but I'll say this much. I have had relationships that have included ageplay and those that have not. But, again, the only relationship I am invested in, one I'm very excited about exploring, is the one we have begun. The one we both committed to last night. Does that help answer your question?"

She nodded. It was reassuring in a way that she hadn't really considered. Looking over, she smiled. "I guess it's a good thing one of us knows what they're doing."

The sound of his chuckle washed over her. "I promise, I not only know what I'm doing, I'm quite anxious to share that knowledge with you. You just need to trust that your daddy will take care of everything. Okay?"

"Okay, Daddy." And with that address, the tension she'd begun to feel evaporated.

A few minutes later, he pulled to a stop, and she looked out the window and then back to him. "Is this your house?"

"No, this is the doctor's office. It's actually shared by several doctors." He turned off the engine, and by the time he'd walked around the car, she had her seatbelt undone and the door open. Though he took her hand and helped her step out, he shook his head. "You need to wait for me to open your door."

"Oh, okay," she said, looking up at the house. "I've never heard of a doctor having his office in a house. And certainly not one like this."

It was a two-story home, set back from the street, the sidewalks bordered by flower beds. A driveway ran up one side, and hanging baskets hung from hooks along the eaves over the railing. As they climbed the steps, she saw some wicker rocking chairs set along the length of the porch. "Wow, this is really pretty." She looked up at him. "Sort of makes you forget what's inside."

"There's no need to be nervous, sweetie. Dr. Harper and his partners all believe in making their patients feel as comfortable as possible."

"Ah, so they don't believe in needles! That's good to know!"

He chuckled and reached to open the door. "Well, there will be needles, but there are also cute Band-Aids and treats for good little girls."

"What about not so good girls?" she asked, furiously

batting her eyelashes and attempting to look innocent.

Grinning, he shook his head. "Cute. But in answer to your question, naughty little girls get treated to a spanking, and they still get their shots when needed," he said as if it was the most normal thing to say, and as she finally looked from him to her surroundings, she figured in this new world she'd stepped into, it most likely was.

The waiting room, which looked far more like a family room, was filled with large, overstuffed armchairs as well as a few settees designed to seat two. There was a colorful area rug in the center of the floor that actually had buildings, houses, and little streets printed on it to allow small toy cars to be driven about the town depicted on the carpet. An oak table sat close to one wall, chairs around it. A shelf next to it contained books and bins of blocks, cards, and crayons just waiting to be chosen by some young patient waiting to see the doctor. The walls were painted a light blue with a border of green depicting grass where large flowers were blooming. It was so unlike the stark doctors' offices she'd visited that she couldn't help but smile... until her eyes caught another shelf, one mounted much higher than the ones the toys and books sat on. It wasn't the fact that several hooks had been mounted along the shelf's edge that had her eyes going wide. It was what hung from those hooks. Paddles of different sizes and material waited to be plucked free and applied to a misbehaving Little's backside. She shook her head. Surely they were for show? Perhaps meant to remind a recalcitrant patient that misbehavior would be frowned upon? No one would actually lift one free and give a spanking to their Little right in the middle of the waiting room, in full view of other people... would they?

For some reason, she felt both a little nervous and curious. Yes, she'd read a few stories on different lifestyles, but she'd never actually seen evidence that any dynamic other than the one deemed 'normal' was actually practiced for real... by real people. She supposed she'd never know as the room was empty but for the two of them.

"Good morning, Mr. Masterson."

The greeting had her eyes darting to the left to see an older woman on the other side of a pass-through window.

"Good morning, Edna," Sawyer said, stepping closer to the woman. "I'd like you to meet Janie. Janie, this is Mrs. Shepherd."

"Hello, Janie, it's very nice to meet you. Feel free to play while your daddy fills out some forms." Edna held out a clipboard with several papers clipped to it.

"Um, that's okay," Jane said. She hadn't missed the fact that this woman had called him by name, which made her wonder exactly how often he'd visited, and with whom. "I can fill them out."

"That's your daddy's job, sweetheart. We have books to read or color in, or, if you prefer, you may choose a toy to play with. I'll let the nurse know you've arrived, Mr. Masterson. You've brought Janie in to see Dr. Harper, correct?"

"Yes, for a baseline physical. Thank you, Edna."

With that, the woman disappeared, leaving Jane to stare up at him. "I don't need a physical. I don't even really need a doctor as I'm perfectly healthy. This is a waste of your time and money."

He ignored both her protest and her attempt to tug her hand free from his. Leading her across the room, he took a seat in one of the chairs, pulling her down onto his lap. "And Daddy said that you will be receiving a physical. We have the time and you need not worry about the cost. As your daddy, it is my responsibility to cover the bill."

"How many other Littles have you brought here?" she demanded when he released her hand in order to take the pen from under the clip so he could begin filling in the forms. His eyes met hers and she snapped, "Don't look at me like that! I have the right to know, and you said I could ask questions!"

"Yes, I did, and you may. But what you may not do, young lady, is speak to me in that tone of voice or with that attitude. I realize you might be a little nervous, but that is no excuse to be rude."

"I'm not nervous! I just think this is stupid, and you still didn't answer me. How do I know you don't have a whole bunch of women just waiting for their own 'Daddy time'?"

"Because I told you that you are the only Little I'm in a committed relationship with, and I do not say things I do not mean. Now, I suggest you lose the attitude and go play before you receive the answer to the question you didn't voice but I know you have."

"What question?"

He cupped her chin with his fingers, gently turning her head in the direction of the receptionist's station. "The one about are those paddles being just for show. I promise you, they are not. And, if you doubt me, I'll be more than happy to choose one, turn you over my knee, and apply it to your bottom until you realize that I do not lie, and I will not tolerate my little girl throwing a fit." He turned her head back gently to face him. Looking down, he asked, "Are we clear?"

Swallowing hard and trying to not clench her buttocks as she was sure he'd find that telling somehow, she nodded.

"Words, Janie. I want to hear you say your words."

"Yes…"

"Yes, what?"

"Yes, sir, we're clear."

"Good," he said, bending forward and kissing her forehead. "Now, go pick a book or a toy and let me fill out your paperwork."

"But what if you don't know the answers?"

"Then I'll ask you." He smiled and the ease with which he lifted her off his lap and set her onto her feet had her frozen for a moment. He was so much bigger, so much stronger than she was. It was both disconcerting and… well, wonderful. When he gave the back of her skirt a pat, she blushed and decided that it wouldn't be all that horrible to go find something to read.

By the time he'd returned the clipboard to the front, not asking Jane for clarification on anything, they were no longer alone. Another man and woman entered and while he was dressed in a suit, the woman's hair was in two pigtails, huge purple bows vivid against the chestnut strands. She wore a lilac-colored dress where another large bow was tied right above the curve of her buttocks. White lacy ankle socks and black Mary Janes completed her outfit. She wasn't that much shorter than the man with her, but her entire persona radiated 'Little'. She smiled and gave Jane a wave. Before Jane could do more than give a lift of her hand in return, the door opened and Edna stepped out.

"Mr. Masterson, Nurse Julie is ready to do the bloodwork."

Sawyer stood up and held out his hand. "Come on, sweetie."

Seeing the other Little's look of empathy, mouthing what looked like 'owie', as well as giving a rather exaggerated shudder, Jane felt torn. She gave a brief look toward the hall that led to the front door, wondering what would happen if she made a break for it. She didn't have a chance to discover the answer because her hand was taken and given a squeeze.

It's just a little bloodwork. You've had blood drawn before and lived through it, remember?

They were led down the hall a bit before turning into a room where a woman met them with a big smile.

"Hi, my name is Nurse Julie." The woman was probably only a few years older than her and Jane wondered what she honestly thought about this entire daddy/little thing. If her cheery voice was any indication, she must think it was just fine. "Are you scared of needles, sweetie?"

"Um... not really, but I don't like getting stuck a lot," Jane said.

"I don't blame you, and I promise I'm very good at what I do. Would you like to climb up on the table or would you rather sit on your daddy's lap while I draw your blood?"

Jane looked at the exam table, which looked like the one

she remembered from her childhood, if a bit taller. Deciding she might as well make the most of what wasn't one of her favorite things, she looked up at Sawyer. "My daddy's lap."

"Good choice," Julie said with a wink. "All right, you get settled, and we'll get started."

Sawyer sat in an armless chair and pulled her onto his lap. "Don't worry," he said, bending to kiss the top of her head. "Nurse Julie is very gentle."

Julie put an elastic band on Jane's upper arm and asked her to make a fist. Doing so, Jane then straightened her arm and pointed to a spot on the inside of her left elbow where the bulge of a vein was visible. "That's where they stuck me last time," she informed the nurse.

"Well, that's a good vein. Thank you, Miss Janie."

Jane knew it was ridiculous, but the woman's words, her tone, and her very smile made her relax and feel proud that she'd helped. It didn't hurt that her daddy was smiling and patting her thigh. The moment the nurse lifted the syringe, Jane's head swam as a memory of watching her blood burbling into the tubes made her feel faint. Enough of this trying to be a grownup shit. With a whimper, she turned her head and pressed her face into her daddy's chest.

"Easy, sweetie, you're being so brave."

His hand running up and down her back took her mind off the fact that another tube was being filled... and another. From the number of tubes taken, she wondered how many tests the doctor was planning to have run.

"All right, all done," Julie said, tucking the tubes away before applying an alcohol swab and placing a cotton ball over the puncture site. Jane was about to hold it in place when her daddy gently lowered his finger to the white piece of fluff.

"Now comes the fun part," the nurse said, moving to the built-in countertop and returning with a basket. "What Band-Aid would you like?"

Choosing a neon pink one with tiny white polka dots, Jane turned to her daddy. "Can you put it on, Daddy?"

"Certainly, honey," he said, applying it and then bending to place a kiss on top of the bandage.

Jumping off his lap, she said, "Thank you, can we go eat now? I'm starving and you promised coffee!"

"No, we're not done. You still need to see Dr. Harper."

Her mouth dropped open. "Oh, right. But the bloodwork is done. I'm sure I have time for a cup of coffee first. Doesn't this office at least have a Keurig?" His shaking head did not make her happy, and neither did Nurse Julie's offer.

"Don't fret, Miss Janie. You've been such a little darling. It's nice to have such a brave and good patient to start my morning. I'll be happy to bring you some juice and a snack after we get your urine sample, honey."

Jane didn't know if that was some sort of praise or subtle warning, but she honestly didn't care. "I don't want juice; I want coffee and a lot of it!"

"Jane, settle down. You are being rude and throwing a fit is not acceptable."

"Neither is breaking your promise!"

"Nurse, would you mind giving us a minute?"

"Certainly."

The moment Julie opened the door, Jane was right behind her. Her squeal of surprise when she was lifted off her feet rang out down the hallway before she was carried back into the exam room and the door shoved closed by her daddy's foot.

"Put me down!"

Her daddy plopped her onto the exam table, instantly caging her in with his arms planted next to her hips, his body leaning toward her so that she had to lean back, her hands splayed against the white paper that covered the table. "You need to calm down, young lady. We've discussed this—"

"We didn't discuss how the hell I'm supposed to pee in some cup when I haven't had anything to drink in forever! I've got to have coffee or at least a Coke!"

"It's quite obvious that you are addicted to caffeine,

which is not healthy. And as far as providing a sample, I assure you that you will be doing so."

"Good luck with that! You can't force me to pee!"

"I would not need or desire to force you to urinate." He paused, his eyes darkening. "You will either be a good little girl and obey Nurse Julie, or Dr. Harper will take the sample himself."

Jane scoffed, "Oh, so *he* will force me—"

"No, Jane, the doctor will simply insert a catheter into your urethra and empty your bladder—"

The very thought of that being a possibility had her bladder clenching and her eyes going wide. "This is-is bullshit! I didn't agree to this!"

"Wrong," he said. "You agreed last night when you accepted me as your daddy."

"I've changed my mind! I don't want a daddy and I don't want to play Little anymore!"

"No? You could have fooled me. You're certainly doing a great job at being a Little. You are throwing a temper tantrum worthy of a spoiled toddler. Last chance—"

"Fuck yo—"

She never got to finish her vulgar curse as he easily lifted her, ignoring the fact that she tore the white paper from the table as she attempted to retain her seat. All she could do was drop the paper and clutch his leg as she was placed over his thigh, his foot propped up on a stool, keeping her well above the floor. Before she could blink, she felt his arm pulling her tightly into his waist. To her horror, he flipped up her skirt, yanked down her panties and his hand slapped down on her bare bottom. Shocked, it took a stroke delivered sharply, and quite loudly, to each globe of her butt before she shrieked, her legs kicking and her hands hammering at his calf. Cracks as loud as gunshots joined the sound of her shrieks as he began to pepper her bottom. It didn't take a half dozen before she whipped one arm behind her, attempting to cover his target.

A bit shocked when the swats stopped, she thought

she'd won until the next swat landed on her right thigh, instantly reminding her that he'd said there were a lot of places where a naughty girl could be spanked. The stroke against her left thigh had her squealing. "I'm sorry! Please, Daddy, not there!"

"Naughty girls who cover their asses get their thighs spanked," he said calmly.

After another pair of swats, she lifted her hand from her bottom and waved it in the air. When he took it, she didn't attempt to pull it free, even when he pinned it to the small of her back.

"I promised to provide for you, take care of all your needs, and be the daddy you've dreamed of forever. I promised not to let you down, not to have you worry about what you can expect. I take my commitments seriously, and, young lady, when you throw tantrums, you get spanked… every single time."

Suddenly, it was like she had an epiphany. This wasn't a dream. Last night's spanking had not been a fluke. The heat she felt all across her nether cheeks easily telegraphed that to be true. The echo of each stroke reverberated around the room and through her very soul. This wasn't some man reluctantly agreeing to give her a few swats after she'd finally gotten up the nerve to beg him and then have him making her feel like some sort of deviant for even suggesting they at least try a little spanking. She was not in control. She'd thrown a fit and he—her daddy—was taking her to task for doing so.

"I'm sorry!" she cried, clinging to his leg with her free hand instead of swatting at it. "Please… stop…"

"Are you going to be my good girl?"

"Yes!" she screeched as each of her poor, burning buttocks was treated to a harder stroke.

"Yes, what?"

"Yes, sir!"

"Are you going to apologize to Nurse Julie?"

"Yes, sir!"

"Are you going to do exactly as the nurse and doctor instruct you?"

"Yes, sir!"

"Are you going to remember that your daddy is committed to you? That he wants nothing more than to assure that his precious girl knows that he will take care of all that she needs?"

"Yes, yes, Daddy!"

"All right. Then we will finish your punishment later."

She felt a little lightheaded as she was flipped upright and set down on her feet. Her daddy pulled her panties back into place and lowered her skirt before lifting her and setting her on his hip until he returned to his original chair, sat, and moved her onto his lap.

Her emotions were churning, and she just couldn't look at him. Instead, she buried her face in his shirt, clutching the fabric.

"Shhh," he said, rocking her in his arms. "You're fine. I've got you."

"You... you really span-spanked me."

"I'm not sure why that comes as a surprise. I spanked you last night."

That was very true, but this was different. Pulling back a bit, her hand waved to indicate the room. "I mean... we aren't in my house. This... this isn't private."

"I told you last night that I would never hesitate to spank you whenever and *wherever* you earned a punishment, remember?"

Well, she couldn't argue with that, but it was as if another level of her new life had just been made crystal clear. She squirmed a bit, the movement doing nothing to ease the sting he'd put into her cheeks. "I blame it on the lack of caffeine," she said, sitting back and looking up at him.

He grinned. "I blame it on the fact that you've been wondering if your daddy really means what he says and if I'd actually call you on your behavior outside the setting of your home or mine."

She could feel her face heat and wondered if it was as red as her ass had to be.

He bent to kiss her forehead. "Now you know that I most definitely will, so no more wondering required."

"I-I guess so," she admitted and then remembered what he had said a few minutes earlier. "What did you mean by we'll finish later?"

He tugged her a little closer before answering. "Part of that you should be able to answer yourself as we discussed it last night." When she didn't immediately answer, he took her hand and laid it against the buckle of his belt.

"But I didn't lie!"

"Didn't you?"

How an arched eyebrow could make her feel like she was either being purposefully obtuse or attempting to deny her guilt, she didn't know, but it did. Her mind raced back to her tantrum and she sighed. "I didn't mean it to be a lie. I just was... was angry."

"A lie is a lie, Janie. Our relationship isn't a game. We're not playing. Granted, it isn't always an easy dynamic, but we have both agreed to it, and you hurt me and yourself when you use that commitment as a weapon."

It was hard to nod, but she had felt awful the moment she'd spewed the denial of her dream to have a daddy. "I'm sorry."

"And there is still the matter of washing your mouth out for the nasty words you uttered."

"I thought after a spanking, it was over. That I was forgiven when you held me."

"You're partially right. You seem to have forgotten that Daddy is the one who decides when the punishment is over and the penance you'll make each time. But, as I said, we will finish it later. And, Janie, know this as well. When Daddy says you will always be forgiven and I will always hold you just like this to make sure you know how very special my baby girl is to me, know that I mean every single word."

She thought about for a moment, remembering the words she'd read on the screen that first night. "Thank you, Daddy."

A few minutes later, a soft knock came on the door and she gasped. "Oh, my God! Everyone is going to know you span-spanked me!"

"No, all the exam rooms are soundproofed, so while Nurse Julie might suspect, and Dr. Harper will know, no one else will."

"Why will he know?"

"Because he'll see your red bottom when he examines you." He gave her a hug, another quick kiss and called out, "Come in."

CHAPTER TEN

Sawyer took the plastic cup from Julie and looked down at Janie. He found the fact that she squirmed and then gave a little gasp very satisfying. He'd been telling her the truth, knowing without a doubt that her little tantrum had been more of a test than an actual fit of pique. Though he had told her, without equivocation, exactly what she could expect whenever she misbehaved, he knew that she'd be over his lap, her adorable bottom bared and reddened many more times before she truly believed he'd follow through every time. And follow through he would as that was what daddies did.

"I want you to take this into the bathroom and..." When she opened her mouth, he shook his head before continuing. "Unless you are about to say, 'yes, Daddy', I suggest you remember that this is the easiest way to provide the sample that the doctor requires."

Another wiggle, another soft mewl, and she accepted the specimen container. "Yes, Daddy."

"That's my good girl. And what would you like to say to Nurse Julie?"

"I'm-I'm sorry for... for being rude."

"And a naughty girl," Sawyer prompted.

DADDY SAYS

Big violet eyes pleaded to be spared the admission, but he didn't budge. With a blush that ran up from the neckline of her yellow blouse to color her cheeks, she watched the nurse pull the ruined paper off the table and replace it with a fresh piece. Jane proved she was very sorry for being so badly behaved by moving off her daddy's lap and bending to pick up the shredded paper on the floor. "And a nau-naughty girl."

"I accept your apology, Miss Janie," Julie said, reaching out her hand after Jane had thrown the paper away. "I'll take you to the bathroom, and after you've finished, you can choose a juice box and a snack."

"Thank you," Jane said, taking the nurse's hand. Sawyer watched as the two left the room, willing to bet that once inside the privacy of the bathroom, Jane would not only fill the container, but she'd take a good long look at her bottom. He smiled, imagining her surprise to discover it wasn't anywhere near as red as she probably thought. It was only her second spanking, and while he hadn't given her love taps, he most certainly had gone easy on her. She'd learn soon enough that a naughty girl's behind could be far more than the rosy hue he'd painted onto her plump little cheeks.

When she returned, sucking on the straw of a box containing apple juice, the gurgling sound attesting to the fact that she'd emptied it rather quickly, he smiled and opened his arms, giving her a hug when she flew into them. "Good juice?"

"It wasn't bad, but it isn't coffee or a Coke," she said softly, leaning against him.

"No, but it is far better for you. Did you eat something?"

"Yes, Jul… Nurse Julie gave me a mini blueberry muffin, but I'm still hungry."

"You can eat a big breakfast after the doctor finishes your exam. And, remember, Janie, you've promised to do exactly as Dr. Harper instructs you—"

"I'm sure she will do just fine." They both looked toward the door to see a man in a white coat, a stethoscope peeking from one pocket, entering. Sawyer kept Janie close with one arm around her waist as he extended his free hand. "Hello, Martin. Thanks for fitting us in today."

"My pleasure, Sawyer. And this must be your Jane."

"Yes, this is Janie. Janie, say hello to Dr. Harper."

"Hello."

"Please, sit down and we'll go over what you can expect."

"Oh, okay," she said, climbing onto Sawyer's lap when he returned to the chair he'd occupied earlier.

The doctor pulled up a wheeled stool and sat down. "As your daddy has probably told you, the purpose of today's visit is to get a baseline on your health. We'll take your height and weight, check your eyes, nose, and throat, your heartbeat, etc. You've had a Pap smear before?"

"Um, no."

Sawyer was surprised and asked, "How did you get birth control without a pelvic exam?"

"The clinic I go to doesn't require one to get the shots," Jane said.

"No, but any doctor will tell you that regular Pap smears are important, and you'll have your first today, young lady," Dr. Harper said. He didn't give her a chance to protest as he asked his next question. "Do you do regular self-exams of your breasts?"

"No, well, not really."

"That's fine. I'll do that as well and show both you and your daddy how to perform them."

Sawyer saw her flush as she snuck a glance up at him, but she didn't protest and turned her attention back to the doctor when he continued. "It's really the same sort of exam you'd receive from your regular doctor. Now, before we begin, do you have any questions or concerns?"

When she shifted on his lap, her fingers playing with the hem of her sweater, Sawyer spoke softly. "Go ahead, sweetie. You can ask whatever you want. It's important that you feel comfortable."

"Really? So if I don't want to do the pelvic thing, I don't have to?"

Sawyer shook his head. "Janie, that question has already been answered. You will have both a pelvic and a rectal exam."

"Daddy!" she squealed, immediately burying her face in his neck.

Giving her a squeeze, he then set her back, but it took his fingers on her chin to have her meeting his eyes. "There is nothing to be embarrassed about. This is a doctor's office, and as I've told you, it is important that we ascertain that you are in good health and capable of playing." He paused and then gave her a grin. "That is if you still want to include sex in our relationship?"

If anything, her face turned even more crimson, but she immediately nodded.

"Then, do you have any other questions?"

"You-you said capable but you know I'm not a virgin. I-I've been capable of having sex for years."

Dr. Harper reached out and patted her knee before sitting back. "What your daddy means is that he is a large man and wants to make sure that your body is capable of handling him without too much discomfort."

Sawyer watched her eyes go huge, drop to his crotch, then fly back to his eyes, a fresh wave of color spreading up her neck.

"What... what if I-I can't?"

Martin continued. "I'm quite sure you can, it just might take a bit of training."

Her eyes darted between the two men and when she didn't speak, Sawyer figured she wasn't quite ready to ask what constituted 'training'. That was fine as she'd learn the answer soon enough.

The doctor stood. "I'm going to step outside. Once your daddy helps you get ready, he can press the button by the table and I'll be back. Just relax, Jane, you're going to be just fine."

He stood and pulled open a drawer under the exam table, pulling out what looked like a short robe. But this wasn't made of paper as seen in most doctors' offices; this was made of soft fabric and instead of sterile white, it was a light pink with a design of baby animals frolicking all over it. Placing the robe on the table, he gave her another smile and then left the room, pulling the door closed behind him.

• • • • • • •

By the time the doctor returned, Jane was seated on the table, her legs swinging a bit. She hadn't had time to worry about how to undress in privacy, because her daddy had done it for her. Her clothes were now neatly folded, waiting on the edge of the counter where he'd put them. He'd put the robe on her, tying the sash in a bow. Asking if she was ready, he assured her that being nervous was fine, but also reminded her that being naughty would be instantly corrected. Once she'd nodded, he pushed the button that would summon Dr. Harper.

"Let's get your weight and height first," the doctor said.

After her daddy lifted her from the table, Jane stepped onto the scales and the exam began. Her weight just tipped the scale at one hundred pounds and though that was within range for her height of 5'2", she giggled when Sawyer seemed a bit shocked and asked if she was seriously underweight.

"No, Sawyer, she is just petite."

"Well, I'll make sure she eats properly," Sawyer said, despite the doctor's assurance.

"How much do you weigh, Daddy?" she asked.

Grinning, he stepped onto the scale and she discovered that her daddy weighed more than double what she did and, as he was 6'3", was a little over a foot taller. No wonder he could lift her so easily! "Wow, you're really big!"

"And you're really little," he countered.

"Are you calling me a little Little?" she teased, squealing

when he not only plucked her off her feet, but tossed her into the air before catching her and returning her to sit on the table.

"I guess I am, but you are an adorable little Little."

The interlude helped ease her nerves and she relaxed as the doctor took her blood pressure and then examined her eyes and ears. It wasn't until he'd pulled on a glove and asked her to open her mouth wide that a bit of nerves returned.

"I'm just going to check your throat, Jane," Dr. Harper said, first shining a light into her mouth and then inserting his fingers far enough that she gagged a bit.

When he removed them, she sucked in a couple of breaths. "My last doctor used a long cotton swab for that," she said.

"That's because he wasn't making sure that you'd be able to accommodate a cock in your throat," Sawyer said, and she practically fell off the table.

"Go on and lie back," Dr. Harper said, as if Sawyer's statement was nothing he was unused to hearing.

"I'm going to check your breasts now," the doctor said, untying the sash of the robe and allowing the fabric to part. "You or your daddy need to do a breast exam every month. If you pick a date and stick to it, it will be easy to remember."

"Oh... okay," Jane said, praying he thought that the room's chill was the cause for her puckered nipples and not the vision that had popped into her head of her kneeling before her daddy, opening her lips to accept his cock. Her burgeoning arousal was helped along when Sawyer's fingers replaced the doctor's after he asked for a far more personal lesson. She tried not to moan or squirm as his fingers palpated each breast, going in slow, ever smaller circles until he actually took her nipple between his thumb and finger and gave it a little squeeze. No one could blame a poor girl for bucking up a bit at that, could they?

"Very good, Sawyer. If you feel any lumps on any part

of her breasts, or there is any discharge, then you need to call me. Other than that, Jane's breasts appear quite healthy." Turning his attention to his patient, Dr. Harper asked, "Have you ever had your nipples clamped before, Jane?"

"No... no, sir," Jane said.

"You have very beautiful nipples, quite prominent for such a little frame, even when they are puckered tightly."

Jane was unsure if she was expected to say anything... thank him for what she was pretty sure was meant to be a compliment but made her blush furiously. She didn't have to speak as he turned his attention to her daddy.

"Sawyer, just remember, since she is unused to clamps, go slowly at first and don't keep them on for very long until she builds up a tolerance. In fact, I'd recommend you begin her training by using your fingers to pinch, pull, and twist her nipples to help her grow accustomed to the pressure and bite of pain before clamping her for the first time."

"I can certainly do that," Sawyer said.

Jane's earlier vision instantly changed. Now she was kneeling—naked, of course—at her daddy's feet, her mouth full of his cock and her nipples aching from the 'training' pinches before he attached clamps onto her tender buds. In her mind, her moans were muffled but audible every time he reached down and gave a clamp a little tug.

"Janie?"

"Huh?"

"Honey, Dr. Harper asked you to scoot your bottom down to the edge of the table."

"Oh... sorry," she said, praying that the grin on his lips was not because he could read her mind. Once she moved down, she gave a little squeal when the doctor pulled her a bit more until she felt as if her butt was hanging off the table.

"It's all right," he said, pulling metal poles out from the table and directing her to place her feet in the stirrups. "You're perfectly safe."

She wasn't really concerned about her safety. She was far more concerned about the fact that thanks to the visions she couldn't seem to stop having, she knew she was a little more than just 'damp' down there. Slamming her eyes shut didn't help as it only seemed to make her vision more vivid.

"Just relax, sweetie, I'm here, and you are doing great," Sawyer said, making her realize that the soft whimpering sound she heard was coming from her.

Still, when he took her hand, she clung to it tightly, and this time when she closed her eyes, she saw herself cuddled on her daddy's lap, his arms holding her close, and a sense of security washed over her. That lasted until she felt fingers sliding along the seam of her sex. Her feet lifted from the stirrups and her thighs began to close.

"No, just remain still," her daddy instructed, his free hand sliding to her inner thigh and pressing gently. "You're fine. Dr. Harper is just checking your vagina. Open your legs."

Jane returned her feet to their proper place and allowed her legs to fall open again.

"I'm going to spread your outer labia open, Jane," Dr. Harper said.

Jane wasn't sure if knowing what he planned to do was any better than being left in the dark, but simply nodded. The fingers returned and though she didn't mean to, she could feel her legs beginning to tremble a bit. "I-I'm sorry," she whispered, not wanting them to think she was being disobedient.

"Nothing to be sorry about," the doctor said. "The vagina is a very sensitive part of your body. It is meant to give you pleasure. Do you masturbate?"

"Um... I-I have, but... um, not anymore," Jane said, her eyes opening to see her daddy smiling down at her.

"Not unless you're given permission?" Dr. Harper asked.

"I-I guess," Jane managed, her stomach muscles tightening as the doctor's fingers began to brush over her clitoris.

"That's quite common in the dynamic. When you do masturbate, do you find it easy to climax?"

"Easy?"

"I mean, does it take a long time to reach your culmination? Do you come from just playing with your clittie or do you use toys as well? A dildo or vibrator in your pussy?"

Jane could feel her entire body heating, from the continual stimulation of her clit and the embarrassment over the question.

"Answer the doctor, please," Sawyer said, giving her hand a squeeze.

"I-I've used a vibrator before, but I've never put it inside my... my vagina. Just used it on my clit at times. I come pretty quickly when I use a vibrator."

"That's pretty normal. Now, just relax. I need to see how you react to stimulation," the doctor said.

At her soft whimper, the doctor removed his finger. "Your daddy is going to bring you to climax so I can assess your sexual arousal." When she looked at him, he grinned and winked. "I believe you'll find this to be a pleasant part of the exam."

"Oh..." she said, a bit mortified that she was going to be forced to come in the presence of another man, but extremely grateful that it would be her daddy bringing her to climax. Just the thought had her pussy spasm, more cream gathering in her sex. She moaned as her daddy's fingers replaced the doctor's. The strokes circled all around her clit.

"Does that feel good?" her daddy asked.

"Yes," she said, having to force herself not to thrust her hips up, wishing he'd be a bit rougher and touch her throbbing button directly.

"How about this?" he asked, granting her silent wish as he rubbed across her clit and then began to give it small taps with his fingertip.

"Oh... yes. Very good."

"I want you to tell me when you are close to coming," Sawyer said, alternating his touches, some soft, some harder, until the spring in her tummy wound tighter and tighter. It didn't take long until she was moaning, her legs trembling.

"I-I'm close," she whispered.

"Then come for me, Jane," her daddy said. "I want you to come now." With that, he pinched her pearl between his finger and thumb, giving it a sharp tug. She arched and moaned, her body jerking as she climaxed.

"Very nice," Sawyer said. He released her clit, giving it a few gentle strokes before removing his hand from between her legs.

"Your pussy provides a nice amount of lubrication," the doctor said, passing Sawyer a moist towelette.

"Is... is that good?" Jane asked, a bit breathless and blushing as her daddy cleaned her essence from his fingers.

"I believe it will prove to be very good," Dr. Harper said. "Your body is providing what you'll need to help accept your daddy easier. And, from the spasms I observed and the fact that you came so quickly, I also believe you are very sensitive and will prove to be multi-orgasmic."

"That will be quite pleasant for you," Sawyer said, bending to kiss her cheek. "That's one advantage of being female."

Jane didn't have the heart to tell him that she doubted his statement. She'd never climaxed more than once before. And while she'd just come rather quickly, that was because she'd already been aroused from the moment he'd pulled her panties down to spank her. Instead, she just smiled and slammed her eyes shut when she saw what the doctor had picked up from a tray.

"Don't be frightened. It's just a speculum. It will be a little uncomfortable, but it's important I check your vaginal walls. Take a deep breath. I'll be done before you know it."

She drew her bottom lip between her teeth to contain her whimper of discomfort as the metal instrument was inserted into her vagina. A moan escaped when he began to crank it open, forcing her inner walls to stretch.

"Relax, baby," Sawyer said, running a finger down her cheek.

Jane wanted to ask for the speculum to be removed, but knew it wouldn't be until the doctor finished his exam. She heard him explain that he was conducting the Pap smear and felt something brush against her deep inside. It wasn't until the speculum released and was removed that she realized she'd been holding her breath. Inhaling deeply, she felt her body shudder a bit.

"You're doing very well," her daddy said.

"Are we done?" she asked hopefully.

"Not quite yet," Dr. Harper said a moment before she flinched as something probed against her anus. "I'm just inserting my finger, first. Have you had anal sex before, Jane?"

How he expected her to talk when he was pushing a finger up her butt, she didn't know, but was very grateful when her daddy answered for her.

"No, she's an anal virgin."

"Okay. If you'll relax and actually push down like you need to go to the bathroom, it will make it easier, Jane."

She really tried, but it was so alien, so embarrassing, that she still clenched and yelped a bit when her sphincter surrendered to the invasion.

"Good girl," Sawyer said, his free hand stroking along her arm. He continued to utter soothing words and give soft strokes as the doctor pulled his finger free. "One more time," Sawyer said softly.

Her yelp was far sharper when the next item was inserted. It was not only larger than the doctor's finger, but cold! She attempted to move back on the table, but her daddy dropped his hand to lie against her tummy.

"No, be still. It's just another speculum."

"I-I don't like it!"

"I know, baby, but it's necessary."

Forgetting about the pleasure she'd just experienced under his hand, all she could think about was the foreign object being forced into a place she'd never considered being invaded. "Have you ever had something pushed up your ass?" she hissed, letting go of his hand in order to use both of hers to push against the table, only to find that she couldn't scoot so much as an inch with his hand splayed against her tummy.

Sawyer bent down, capturing her eyes with his. "I know it's uncomfortable, but you will be a good girl and be still and let Dr. Harper finish his exam." He paused and then added, "Unless you'd rather have another spanking first?"

She'd actually totally forgotten about that spanking, and his tone told her he'd have no problem whatsoever in flipping her over and reddening her butt. Shaking her head, she stopped attempting to get away. His eyes softened as he bent to kiss her forehead and took her hand again. She whimpered as the speculum was opened, expanding to a width that had her squeezing her daddy's fingers as hard as she could.

"It's too much, Daddy."

"Shhh, I know it feels that way, but, baby girl, your body is capable of adjusting. Just a few more minutes and you'll be done." He slipped a hand to her sex, his fingers feathering lightly over it. Looking down at her, he grinned. "And, uncomfortable or not, your pussy is getting even wetter."

She knew her face was scarlet, yet couldn't deny his statement. Just thinking about why she was on this table, why she was being subjected to such an uncomfortable, embarrassing exam, was evidently enough for her body to betray her. When the instrument was finally slid from her, her daddy also removed his fingers. She was allowed to remove her feet and Sawyer helped her to sit up again.

"I know that wasn't pleasant," Dr. Harper said, removing his gloves and giving her a smile. "But, your daddy is right. An exam is necessary and nobody has ever actually died from embarrassment, I promise. Why don't you get dressed and then we will meet in my office?"

He left but when she began to climb down, her daddy shook his head. "Not yet. Go ahead and lie back again."

"Why?" she asked.

"First because Daddy said to and second, because if I put you back into your panties before cleaning you up, you'd be uncomfortable."

"Oh," she said, lying back and watching him pull several towelettes from the container on the counter. She squirmed a bit at the thought of what he intended to do, but when he instructed her to open her legs, she obeyed.

"Good girl," he said, using the wipes to remove not only the lube the doctor had used, but her own cream as well. He bent and gave her pussy a quick kiss that threatened to have her pussy gushing again.

"Daddy, if you don't stop, we'll never get my panties on."

Sawyer laughed and after tossing the towels into the trash, plucked her off the table, not immediately setting her down, but taking a moment to hold her.

"You did very well for your first exam, Janie," he said, giving her a soft kiss.

"I-I moved—"

He nodded. "You did, but for someone who avoids doctors like the plague, I'd say you did an excellent job."

"So I'm as healthy as I said?" she asked a bit petulantly.

"Yes, I'm pretty sure you are, but we'll wait for the doctor to give his concurrence. Do you have any other questions?"

She could feel her face heat, but she had to know. "Do... do you think I'm... capable?"

"Capable?"

Okay, her face now felt like a furnace, but she still needed to know. "I mean, isn't that what this was about? Seeing if my size is going to keep us from... you know, having sex?"

"I'm quite positive we will be cleared for sex, but this was about making sure you were healthy enough to have the kind of sex I want to teach you."

"What kind is that?"

"Anal, oral, vaginal, often and sometimes quite hard, especially if I fuck you as part of a punishment. Does that scare you?"

Her nipples were like bullets beneath the robe and as her heart was pounding, new visions of what they'd be doing together flashing through her mind. She answered honestly. "Yes, a little, but... not enough to run."

Sawyer laughed. "I'm very glad to hear that." After he dressed her, they left the exam room. Dr. Harper confirmed that she was a very healthy young woman and that though both her vagina and anal canal were very tight, with a bit of training and a bit of restraint, they should have no trouble enjoying a healthy sex life.

"Do you have any questions?" Dr. Harper asked, closing her file and smiling at her.

Giving her daddy a look, Jane returned her gaze to the man who had turned out to be pretty nice and who'd not said a single word about her pink bottom during the exam. "I read somewhere that a person should not swallow soap. That soap is actually considered poisonous."

The doctor chuckled. "I'm guessing that someone is worried about having her mouth washed out?"

Jane shifted a bit on her daddy's lap, but valiantly continued. "I just wanted to know if that's true. I mean, you're a doctor and took the Hippocratic oath about doing no harm, so if you knew that maybe one of your clients was... um, going to poison someone, even accidentally, you'd have to tell them not to, right?"

Dr. Harper nodded. "I most certainly would, but I don't think you have a thing to worry about, Jane."

Turning to look at her daddy, Jane said, "Did you hear that, Daddy? Dr. Harper said it's not safe to wash my mouth out."

"No, that's not what he said, young lady. He said you don't need to worry when I do wash your mouth out," he corrected, his eyes twinkling a bit. "And he's right, you don't need to worry your pretty little head about being poisoned as I won't be using soap."

She didn't have time to really consider his words as he was setting her onto her feet and shaking the doctor's hand. Jane walked beside her daddy through the waiting room, surprised to find it crowded. It was clear that there were far more people who lived a different sort of life, enjoyed the dynamic of ageplay than she'd imagined. When she saw another young woman who looked quite nervous, Jane smiled and gave her a little wave.

As they left the house, Jane was about to pull the wrapper off the grape lollipop she had been given for being a 'good patient' when her daddy plucked it from her fingers.

"Hey! I earned that!" she said.

He slipped the candy into his pocket. "You also earned something else, didn't you, little girl? I'm afraid any treat will have to wait until your punishment is completed."

Jane looked up at him to find his expression seemed to be a mixture of anticipation and determination. As he helped her into the car and fastened her seatbelt, she asked, "I thought since you... um, let me come, that the punishment was really over."

"Your climax was part of your exam and does not negate the need for me to complete your lesson."

"Does that mean no coffee or breakfast either?"

Sawyer's smile should have reassured her, but the look and the finger that he lifted to run along the seam of her lips had her breath catching in her throat. "I'm not going to let you starve, sweetie, but I believe you'll be grateful not to have anything on your stomach for a bit longer."

"Why?"

"Because after I give you your whipping for lying, I'll be washing those naughty words out of your mouth. And while I won't be using soap, you might wish I were." As if sensing her confusion, he continued. "I'll be using a totally natural ingredient, and it will come from my cock as I fuck your throat."

CHAPTER ELEVEN

Jane did not seem to be aware of their entry into the building, his introduction of the doorman or the elevator ride to the top floor. She'd been quiet on the drive to his place, her shifting in her seat and futile glances in his direction telling of her nervousness.

Sawyer took her purse and helped her out of her sweater, laying both on a table in the foyer. Once in the living room of his apartment, Jane also seemed not to notice the floor-to-ceiling windows making up an entire wall, showcasing the city below them. When she wasn't looking down at her feet, she was sneaking peeks at the belt around his waist, or darting glances at his crotch.

That was fine. There would be plenty of time for a tour later. For now, it was time to move forward. She needed to learn that she could count on his words and that every time she chose to be naughty, she would pay a price. This punishment would be more intense than the two spankings she'd received so far. While he could commiserate, he had no intention of not starting off the way he would continue. He knew of a sure-fire way to draw her out of her semi-trance.

"Pull your panties down."

Her head snapped up, her eyes widening. "Wha-what?"

"You heard me. Reach beneath your skirt and pull your panties down."

It took her a moment, but she obeyed, blushing furiously as she lowered her panties, looking up at him when they reached her knees.

"All the way down," he instructed and once they were at her ankles, she straightened, her hands now holding her skirt to her sides as if afraid some nonexistent gust of wind would blow it up and expose her bare bottom.

It took only a minute to roll his sleeves up to his elbows, her eyes watching every single fold of the cloth. "Do we need to discuss why Daddy is going to take off his belt and whip you soundly?" he asked, reaching for his belt buckle.

Her breath hitched as she lifted her eyes to his, her mouth opened and yet she finally just shook her head. That would not do as he wanted her directly participating.

"I expect a verbal response, young lady."

"No... no, Daddy. I-I know why."

"All right then." Pulling the leather free in one smooth movement, he wasn't surprised to hear her soft mewl. Naughty young ladies quickly learned that the whoosh of a belt being removed equated with it being used against their bare little bottoms. Sawyer slowly folded the belt in half and held it against his thigh. "Go bend over the arm of the couch."

Her feet shuffled and her eyes remained on the belt. "Please... I-I'm sorry, Daddy."

"I'm sure you are. Now do as Daddy says and bend over the couch. Lift your skirt and present your bare bottom to Daddy."

She'd learn that he believed that it helped put her in the proper mindset when he made her prepare herself for her punishment, even having to bring him various implements when instructed. By the time they were done, she'd have no illusions that she hadn't been naughty or that her daddy was going to allow her behavior to go unpunished.

He watched as she slowly shuffled to the large leather sofa, looking back over her shoulder when she'd reached it, her hesitancy obvious.

"If I have to ask you again to position yourself, you'll get additional strokes against your thighs."

With a soft cry, she reached behind to tug her skirt up to her waist and then practically threw herself over the well-padded arm of the couch. Sawyer grinned to see that she kept her hands cupped over the lobes of her bottom as if attempting to hide her nakedness. While it was absolutely precious, it also meant she was still not fully obeying him.

Sawyer stepped forward. "Is this how I instructed you to present, Janie?"

Her head turned back and she began to nod. When he simply quirked his eyebrow, the nod became a reluctant shake. "What did Daddy tell you he wanted to see?"

"My... my bare bottom."

"That's correct and yet I'm seeing your hands instead." He could see her reluctance as she slowly slid her hands off her ass. "Put your hands under your chest or down into the cushions as I don't want to accidentally strike them. Lay your face down, stick your bottom out." Once she obeyed, he placed his palm against the small of her back. "Six strokes, Janie. I want you to count each one and let the bite of my belt remind you that Daddy does not allow his precious girl to lie... not to him and not to herself. Understand?"

"Ye-yes, Daddy."

Lifting his arm, he swung, the belt catching her directly across the center of her bottom. She squealed, attempting to rear up, but his hand kept her in place.

"Give me a number, Janie, or the stroke won't count."

"One!" she said instantly.

"Good girl." The second stroke was delivered an inch beneath the first.

Her feet kicked up and her cry was louder as the line bloomed against her skin. "Two!"

The crack of leather meeting bare flesh was distinctive... one heard over centuries when little girls or errant wives were being reminded that naughtiness had a price. The third stroke had her jerking her hips to the side.

"Three! Daddy, please! No more!"

"Three more, Janie. Settle and keep your bottom lifted. Come on, little one, I know you can do this."

When her striped bottom lifted, he delivered the fourth and fifth, and though she bucked and screeched, she gave the proper count.

"Last one, but know that if we have to address lying again, the count will not be so light."

The last stroke was delivered to caress her sweet spot, causing her to kick up both feet, her hands drumming against the sofa cushion, her head arching back as she screamed. He gave her a moment, knowing her ass was on fire. "Number, honey."

"Si-six."

Sawyer rubbed his palm over her hot cheeks. Though he was pretty sure she thought he'd skinned her alive, he knew the welts would disappear within a couple of hours and there would be no bruising. He helped her rise, biting back a grin when she immediately threw her hands behind her, rubbing furiously as she bounced around. He knew he should forbid her from attempting to soothe her bottom, but her little 'hot bootie' dance was just too adorable. Instead, he threaded his belt back around his waist and then reached for her, leading her to the front of the couch. Taking a seat, he guided her to stand between his legs.

"On your knees."

She knelt, her eyes locking onto his hand as he reached to unbutton and unzip his pants. Pulling his cock free, he fisted it in one hand while reaching to cup her chin with the other.

"Little girls who choose to spew filthy words get their mouths washed out. Open."

Janie again swallowed hard but her lips obediently

parted.

"One day you will suck my cock for both your pleasure and mine, but this is punishment, Janie. It won't be easy. Daddy is going to fuck your mouth hard. You will accept the correction and will swallow every drop I give you. Understand?"

"I-I don't do this very... very well," she said softly, her face going crimson.

"We can work on technique later," he said. "Right now all I want you to think about is that Daddy will not allow his precious girl to be vulgar. Now, open your mouth and stick your tongue out."

· · · · · · ·

Jane was quite sure that there was no way his cock was going to fit in her mouth. He was huge! Far larger than any man she'd ever dated. He was also far sterner, far more confident, absolutely certain that she'd obey him. And though her ass burned, the whipping having taken her very breath away, she obediently parted her lips. Shame suffused her as she stuck her tongue out, already very, very sorry she had cursed.

Her daddy moved to thread his fingers in her hair, fisting strands close to her scalp, instantly and silently informing her that she was not the one in control. Her hands moved to splay against his thighs as he guided his cockhead to lie on her tongue. When she bent forward to take him into her mouth, the fist in her hair pulled her back.

"No, you aren't pleasuring or worshipping my cock. You will do exactly as I say and only as I say."

She couldn't answer as he hadn't pulled her back far enough to break the contact between her tongue and his cock.

"Keep your eyes on mine," he said, and once she'd lifted hers, he slid his cock back and forth along her tongue. It should have been humiliating but for some reason, that wasn't the emotion that flowed through her. Instead, she could feel submission consume her even as moisture slipped out of her, gathering in the folds of her sex.

Sawyer smiled and as if understanding that she was ready, if ignorant of what was expected, he placed his free hand against her throat and her pussy gushed.

"You will feel as if you can't breathe, but know that I will not take you further than you can go."

For some reason, his words and the hand on her throat weren't threatening... they were settling. How she trusted him with her very breath, she didn't know, but she did. With a nod, he slid forward, filling her mouth inch by inch. Her lips begin to close but when he shook his head, she opened them again—the desire to suck, to lick, to taste overwhelming, but the desire to obey, to atone, was stronger, allowing her to simply be the vessel, the cock sheath he required.

That was her last coherent thought as her punishment began. With a thrust, he pressed against the back of her throat, withdrew and thrust forward again. It was sudden, it was demanding, and as she fought not to gag, she understood why she'd not been allowed to eat or drink.

This was nothing like any blowjob she'd ever given. His cock completely filled her mouth, stretching her lips to a point she was sure was obscene-looking. Drool slipped from her mouth as she attempted to grab breaths whenever he pulled back to allow it. Her eyes watered until he was nothing but a blur. Her fingers dug into his thighs and the sounds coming from her filled the room as he did exactly what he'd promised and fucked her face.

His bulbous head continued to push against her throat, demanding she accept him. She'd never once had a man push into her throat, never imagined they'd be able to, but there was nothing she could do to avoid her daddy's entry. He held himself still until she began to panic, pushing against his legs.

"No," he said sternly, not pulling back until she relaxed

her hands. He retreated a bit, teaching her that she could breathe shallowly with her mouth full of him and then withdrew completely, his cock slick with her saliva as she gulped large lungfuls of air.

"What was that naughty word you said?"

God, she didn't want to say it... not now when she knew that doing so would earn her his cock cutting off her very breath. She shook her head, her eyes pleading not to have to answer and yet he arched his eyebrow and waited.

"Fu-fuck," she whispered. "But, I'm sorry! I won't ever say it again, I swear!"

"I never want to hear that word out of you unless we are in bed and it is said in passion. Understand?"

"Yes, Daddy. I'm so sorry."

He nodded, his hand stroking up and down his impossible length. "Open."

With a whimper, she licked her lips and, like the good girl she was so trying to be, she opened her mouth wide and he began again.

Jane had no idea how long she was on her knees. She only knew that her world consisted of nothing but her daddy's cock. She gagged, her stomach rebelled, her lungs complained, and yet he didn't stop until with a final few, deep thrusts, he pulled back a fraction.

"Every drop," he said a moment before his cock jerked, sending a flood of his seed into her mouth and down her throat. It was far too much for her to accept even though she tried, swallowing convulsively, but still some of his cum slipped from her lips.

"Suck and clean me."

She obeyed, her tongue swirling around his cock, licking up his shaft and across the head that had battered the back of her throat.

"Open," he said.

When she obeyed, he withdrew his cock and for some unfathomable reason, she instantly missed having it commanding her, controlling her, dominating her. When he swiped a finger across her chin and then presented a bit of semen she'd missed to her lips, she instantly opened her mouth wide, her tongue darting out to accept the gift.

"Such a good girl," he said, the praise warming her. Her throat ached, her ass throbbed, but when he reached to pull her up, settling her on his lap, she couldn't think of a single place she'd rather be.

"I'm sorry, Daddy."

"I know, baby girl, but it's over. You did very well in accepting your punishment. All is forgiven and you have a clean slate. I'm proud of you, Janie."

"You are?"

"Yes, little one. The question is, are you ever going to say you don't want to be here, doing this, having me as your daddy?"

She shook her head. "I'd rather learn to suck you for pleasure than have you wash my mouth out again," she said, her face heating as she tried to picture how she must have looked. "But, I can't imagine not having you as my daddy."

He hugged her hard, bending to kiss her, shocking her that he didn't seem to care that his scent had to be on her lips, his seed still coating the mouth that his tongue was now sweeping. His hand patted against the welts he'd placed on her bottom, and she knew that every word she'd spoken was the truth. Breaking the kiss, he gave her another hug and then said, "I promised Dr. Harper to make sure you receive proper nutrition. How about some breakfast?"

"Do we have to go out? I'd rather stay here with you, Daddy."

He smiled and gave her bottom another pat. "Let's go see what I can whip up in the kitchen."

Jane grinned and squirmed a bit at the word 'whip'. "I'd love to cook breakfast for you, Daddy."

He shook his head. "Daddy is supposed to take care of you, little one, not the other way around."

"But I love to cook. I've been saving to go to culinary school and it would be good practice. Please, Daddy?"

Her daddy lifted her up and onto her feet. "How about we cook together?"

"Yes!"

"All right then, let's get you dressed and raid the kitchen."

She was a bit surprised when he had to stoop down to pick up her panties as she'd had no idea they'd come off, most likely when she'd been kicking during her whipping. As she lifted her feet to step into them and he pulled them up her legs, she blushed, hoping he wouldn't realize how wet she was. She'd been being punished and was pretty sure she wasn't supposed to be aroused.

When his hand cupped her sex, his finger stroking over her clit, she moaned.

"You're a very wet little girl, aren't you?"

"Ye-yes, sir, I'm sorry."

"Don't be," he said, giving her cunny a pat before removing his hand to finish pulling her panties over her bottom. "It makes Daddy happy to know that his little one is ready for him even when her bottom has been set on fire."

"Oh," she managed, wishing he'd do something about the other fire just being with him kindled, but remembered what he'd said about not allowing pleasure after a punishment. Taking his hand, she knew she'd gladly give up an entire pot of coffee if only he'd lift the ban and allow her to feel her daddy filling her pussy with his cock as he'd done her mouth.

CHAPTER TWELVE

The kitchen was a chef's dream come true. Stainless steel appliances gleamed amid black countertops, weathered gray planks covered the floor and a pattern of gray, white, and red tiles of the backsplash beneath pristine white cabinets gave the entire room a clean and welcoming feel. Janie had practically swooned at the sight of a professional grade coffee machine, clapping her hands and bouncing on the balls of her feet as he loaded it with beans. The aroma as they ground with a push of a button had her inhaling deeply.

"You really are a coffee addict, aren't you?" Sawyer teased.

"Guilty as charged," she admitted. Tearing her eyes away from the liquid dripping into the carafe, she smiled up at him. "Your kitchen is awesome. I'd never want to go out when I could cook right here."

Unhooking a gleaming copper skillet from the rack above the six-burner range, he grinned. "I'll confess that while I can throw a simple meal together, I usually leave all the cooking to Mrs. West." Setting the pan down, he continued, "And, if I hadn't gone out, I wouldn't have found you. Now, how about omelets?"

Coffee forgotten, she had frozen the moment he

mentioned Mrs. West. He had a driver, a doorman who greeted him by name, lived in a building that bore his name on the outside. Of course he'd have a cook. No man as successful and busy as he would do his own cooking and cleaning. Was someone else in the apartment with them? She'd not yet seen the whole apartment but knew it had to be huge as it took up the entire top floor of the building.

"Janie? What's wrong? You don't like omelets?"

"Did they hear you whipping me?" she asked, her hands going behind her as if to hide the evidence of her punishment. "Oh, God, did they see me... me sucking your... your cock?" Her hands flew to her mouth, her chest tightening at the thought of her intimate, humiliating discipline being witnessed by strangers.

Sawyer had her pulled to him before she finished her question, one arm wrapped around her, his free hand cupping her chin, tilting her head back so that she had to meet his gaze. "Breathe, Janie. Just breathe. I've got you." Taking deep breaths himself, he continued to speak softly, soothingly until she managed to drag in a deep lungful of air and release it in a shuddering exhale. After she'd taken another, he said, "No one is here besides us."

"Thank... thank God," she gasped, only to feel her breath stick in her throat when he continued.

"That's not to say that someday someone on my staff won't be in the apartment when we are. Mrs. West is both my cook and housekeeper and is here every day at some point. Honey, breathe. I promise you that you have nothing to worry about."

"You... you can't do that again. Not where someone could see," she said, attempting to shake her head but only able to make a small movement as he still held her chin. "I'd die if someone knew what... what we did."

"No, little one, you won't die. And neither do you need to fret. My staff has been vetted, and I do not hire anyone who doesn't have an understanding about the dynamic in which I live my life. And while I will never do anything to purposely cause you embarrassment, I will not guarantee that won't happen. Every room in this place belongs to me. Every piece of furniture." He paused and before she knew it, she found herself being lifted and set onto the counter of the huge island. "Every countertop, every surface, and, little one, if I want to push up your skirt and take off your panties, they'll come off." Yanking her skirt from beneath her bottom, he pushed it up before reaching to pull those very panties down her legs, tossing them to the floor. "If I want to spread your legs, they'll be spread." Large hands guided her legs apart, fingers stroking her inner thighs.

Her quivering increased when he bent, his lips kissing the pale skin, his breath warming the flesh that had broken out in goosebumps. His eyes—those gorgeous eyes the color of the ocean—mesmerized her as much as his smile and his words did as he continued.

"If I tell you to lie back, to show me your beautiful pussy, to display how very wet you are… to put your arms above your head so that I can taste the sweet cream I can see filling your slick folds, then I shall expect you to obey." He bent forward and kissed her gently, stroking a fingertip along the pulse at her throat. His lips moved to her cheek, her forehead, her neck as his fingers worked the buttons of her blouse. The only noise was her soft whimper when he unhooked her bra, pushing both it and her blouse off her shoulders, freeing her breasts and exposing nipples that were already puckered and going tighter as he gazed at them, his thumbs brushing over the taut buds. "Lie back, Janie."

She shouldn't obey, she should be worried about someone seeing, thinking she had to be some kind of little slut, and yet she was soon on her back, not resisting when his hands guided her arms above her head, linking her fingers together. She didn't resist when he unzipped her skirt and pulled it off, leaving her totally naked. Not a single muscle protested when he lifted her feet, planting them on the chilled marble, pushing them up toward her bottom and then pressing her thighs down until she was open, displayed before him like a carnal offering.

"If I have to bare your bottom and punish you, if I have to wash your mouth out with my cock when you've been my naughty little one, I will. If I want to feast, to lick and nibble every inch of my precious girl, then I will. And, Janie, if I want to bend you over, or pull you onto my lap or spread you wide to fuck you, then nothing and no one will stop me because you are mine and, little one, I am yours. Any questions?"

"No… no, Daddy." Her next sounds weren't words, but a gasp as his lips settled on her clit and he suckled hard, drawing the entire pulsing bud into his mouth, his tongue lashing over her pearl as her hips lifted, offering him whatever he desired. Was she a horrid person for no longer caring if someone saw her? Was she wanton for allowing nothing but sensation to fill her mind as he took what he wanted… when and where he desired? If so, then so be it. She'd waited her entire life to experience this, to feel both desired and protected, punished and pleasured, to finally be able to simply let go… to allow her daddy to be in control.

"So beautiful," he murmured, lifting his head, his lips glistening from the cream her body continued to provide. "You're going to come for me, Janie. You're going to be a good girl and come very hard for Daddy, aren't you?"

She nodded, her teeth biting her bottom lip as he slid a finger into her, gliding it in and out of her sheath.

"And then you are going to come again," Sawyer said, his grin and the absolute surety of her obedience shone in his eyes. The spring inside her coiled tighter, her nipples protruding toward the ceiling, her body quivering, her pussy spasming and when his lips returned, she knew that she was going to disappoint him when he discovered she couldn't come twice… not as close together as he seemed to want, but his tongue thrusting into her pussy made it impossible to warn him.

When she shattered, her entire body jerked, her hands unlocking from each other to grasp his head, fingers pulling against dark strands, the sensation too much. He didn't allow her to move him a single centimeter from his goal, his tongue delving deep inside her to lap at her nectar, a hand lifting to settle on a nipple, the pinch causing her to squeal, her body bucking again.

"Oh, God," she moaned, never before feeling as if every single cell in her body was alive, on fire as his lips, tongue, and mouth continued to consume her. "Daddy… please, I-I can't!"

"Yes, baby girl, you can, and you will," he countered, lifting his head only long enough to speak. "Because do you know what will happen if you don't?"

"No… no, sir."

He grinned, broadening his tongue and giving her a long, slow swipe from her clit, through the seam of her sex, across her taint, only to stop on the small pucker of her anus, causing her to clench his hair tighter, her mind reeling as he ran the tip of his tongue around the wrinkled rim.

"If you don't come again, then Daddy is going to have to spank this little cunny and this precious little pucker until they are hot and red and you are begging me to give you another chance to obey. Is that what you need, Janie? Do you need me to make your pussy and pucker burn like I did your bottom?"

She couldn't believe that part of her wanted to say 'yes, Daddy', that her pussy was convulsing already at the thought of his hand smacking down on her tender folds. What would it feel like to have her buttocks spread so that he could spank her so intimately between them? Even as she wondered, she was vigorously shaking her head.

"No-no, Daddy," she said, having to release her hold on her bottom lip to answer. "I don't mean to be naughty. I just meant that I've never come twice before."

He arched his eyebrow as if giving her confession no weight. "If you don't want a cunny spanking, if you don't want your pucker paddled, then what are you going to have to do?" The question was immediately followed by him reversing the path he'd taken, dragging his tongue back up to hover above her clit. "Tell Daddy, Janie. What are you going to have to do to be my good girl?"

"Co-come again, Daddy."

"Come how?" he asked, giving her clit a single flick of his tongue.

"Hard. I-I have to come hard."

"That's right. Come so hard that you feel as if you are flying. Now put your hands back and keep them there. Move them again and Daddy will have to punish you."

Reluctantly, she untangled her fingers from his hair, once again putting her arms above her head and locking her fingers together. It was like untying the mooring line of a boat and she felt adrift, out of control, her choice of destination removed from her. Sure that she'd soon discover exactly what that punishment would entail, she felt her pucker clench even tighter, her pussy convulsing as if knowing that pain would replace the pleasure she'd felt.

"That's my good girl. Daddy's got you," he praised, splaying her legs a bit wider, his words assuring her that she was not going to drift far—that he was the captain of this vessel. "Let go, Janie. Don't worry about anything, just feel and let yourself fly."

He drew sounds from her that she'd never uttered before. Mewls, groans, gasps, grunts, and pleas as he set her on fire in a totally different way. The fingers of one hand plucked, tweaked, and twisted her nipples, never faltering as he moved between the two, easily finding each beaded bud to torture it until she was writhing, her back arching, offering her breasts to him. Teeth grazed her clit, scraping the sensitive button before soothing it with long licks and deep suckles. Her fingernails dug into tender palms, as his finger entered her, followed by another and a third, filling her, and when he finally released her nipple to slide a finger between her cheeks, the tip pressing against an entrance she'd always considered something dirty... taboo, she held her breath as the spring inside her coiled tighter and tighter as he slowly, but steadily worked his finger into her ass. Every nerve ending in her dark channel wakened as he stroked against the flesh. She moaned, her body his to do with as he wished and when his fingers began to pump in and out of her pussy, a second finger joining the one in her ass, his tongue licking, teeth nipping, she threw back her head and keened. Every movement pushed her to new heights, had her body tensing, her muscles tightening, and when she reached the breaking point, she screamed and flew apart, every muscle contracting, releasing, only to contract again.

"Absolutely beautiful," Sawyer said, changing the angle of his fingers, pressing against the soft spongy area of her G-spot. Despite her mewls, her writhing, he didn't slow his movements, as if determined to pull every last contraction from her, making her whimper and twist on the countertop. "That's it, baby, give it all to Daddy."

Impossibly, she felt another wave of intense pleasure sweep through her and then arched and screamed as something deep inside let go, exploded within her, causing fluid to gush from her body. "Daddy!" she screamed, her hands unlocking as she tried to push herself up, only to realize she was too boneless to move.

"Shhh, shhh," he said, finally allowing his movements to begin to slow. "It's all right."

"But… but I wet myself!" She squeezed her eyes shut, knowing she'd never be able to look him in the eyes again.

"Janie, look at me."

She shook her head, tears welling.

"Baby, open your eyes and look at Daddy." It took his finger stroking down her cheek before she could obey. Once she did, she saw such passion and love in his eyes that she didn't immediately slam hers shut again. "Janie, you didn't wet yourself. You squirted."

She could feel her entire body heating, her lips trembling as that sounded even more horrific than wetting herself. "I-I'm sorry. I-I didn't…"

"No, sweetheart, it was beautiful. It means you trusted me enough to let go, to allow me to teach you to fly. Tell me, how did it feel?"

Jane didn't answer immediately, her mind replaying the most incredible orgasm of her life, her body still giving off little shockwaves in the aftermath, and she realized it had been... well, indescribable as she had absolutely nothing to compare it to. Looking at him, she whispered, "Amazing. Really... really amazing."

He smiled and bent over her, lowering his mouth to a fraction of an inch above hers. "You are amazing, Janie. You flew, little one."

"I-I guess I did," she admitted, barely having time to smile before his mouth crushed hers. She wrapped her arms around his neck, holding him close as he kissed her until she couldn't breathe. When he pulled back, she said, "Thank you, Daddy."

"Thank you, Janie, thank you for being the most amazing woman I've ever known." He kissed her again and then helped her to sit.

"Oh, God, this is... um... messy." She could feel the fluid she'd released beneath her bottom and thighs.

"No worries," Sawyer said, not giving her time to be embarrassed as he stepped away, returning with a cloth he'd wet beneath the faucet. He lifted her to move a foot away and then gently washed her, causing fresh goosebumps to pop out on her skin as he ran the warm cloth over her sensitive flesh. Once she was clean, he wiped down the countertop, removing every trace of her fluid before turning to her and plucking her off the counter. When she bent to retrieve her scattered clothing, he stayed her with a hand on her arm. "No, baby." She watched as he unbuttoned his shirt and then smiled as he helped her into it. "I'd keep you naked but you're so skinny I'm afraid you'll not stop shivering." The shirt hung on her as he buttoned it up, taking the time to give each of her nipples a quick kiss before finishing the task. As he rolled the sleeves up, she shuddered, her bottom clenching as she remembered him doing so before he'd pulled off his belt. After he was done, he dropped a kiss on top of her head.

"Now, where were we? Oh, yes, I was asking if you knew how to make omelets."

"I do," she said, moving toward the counter. "But first, if I don't have a cup of coffee, I just might die."

He laughed and after they'd both taken a few sips of those first cups, she finally opened the refrigerator. "Oh, wow, this is going to be such fun."

· · · · · · ·

They ate out on the balcony, high above the street. She sat opposite him, her bare feet curled up beneath her. The slight breeze lifted her hair, sending curls across her face, which he would reach over to tuck behind an ear. The omelets were delicious, the bacon crisp, the toast perfectly done, and the coffee plentiful.

"We are going to have to cut down on your caffeine intake," he said as she emptied her mug for the fourth time. "You've practically drank an entire pot."

"Just one?" she teased, causing his eyebrow to arch. "I usually have two or three pots a day."

"That's going to come to a screeching halt," Sawyer said, shaking his head. "No way any doctor is going to consider that good."

"But I'll get very cranky," she pouted.

"Crankiness I can correct," he assured her, moving a glass of orange juice to replace her coffee mug. "You can start with a blend of half-regular, half-caffeinated—"

"Why bother? Decaf isn't the same."

"Of course, we could also just put a total ban on coffee altogether," he suggested, though she knew it could easily become more than a suggestion.

Or we could just get a brand-new daddy, she thought but instantly knew she'd never want another man—not when she'd been blessed to find the perfect daddy dom. "Um, no, that's okay. We'll try it your way."

"I thought so," he said with a grin. "Now, finish your orange juice and then we need to go over a few things."

"Yes, Daddy," she said, lifting her glass. When she had drained it, they cleared the table, putting the dishes in the sink. "I can do them," she said, feeling bad about leaving them undone.

"No, we have far more important things to do," Sawyer countered, taking her hand and leading her from the kitchen.

They wound up sitting on the same couch she'd bent over before, but this time she was on his lap. Though he didn't have a laptop, he seemed to remember every single answer she'd given on his questionnaire and they discussed them for several minutes.

"So, I get to pick a safeword?" she asked.

"Yes, but know that it only comes into play when, well, we are playing," he said. "When you are being punished, there is no safeword."

"But what if it is too much?"

"You've been punished already. You've received both a spanking and a whipping as well as having had your mouth washed out. Was any of that too much?" He gave a grin when she instantly opened her mouth, placing a finger across her lips before she could answer. "Remember, those strokes with my belt were for lying, so consider your answer carefully."

"Oh… um, then, no," she said with a sigh. "I didn't like them, but… they weren't too much."

"Good girl," he said, giving her a squeeze. "I will never take you further than you can go, Jane. That's not to say I won't take you farther than you might believe or want to go, but you can trust that I'll never harm you."

"That seems a bit unbelievable when my butt still hurts."

"Hurt is different than harm. Punishments aren't meant to be pleasant and your ass or wherever I've punished for your transgressions should hurt for a bit. But that hurt will go away. There will never be any lasting harm, either physically or emotionally. Does that make sense?"

She considered it a moment and then nodded. "I guess, but how do you know how far I can go?"

"I observe and your body's reaction tells me just as much, if not more, than the sounds you make or the look in your eyes. Tell me. When I first ordered you to open your mouth and stick out your tongue, did you believe you'd be able to take my cock into your throat?"

Heat rushed through her, her eyes dropping to look down his bare chest to where a line of dark hair began beneath his belly button as if pointing the way to the cock in question. "Um, I-I didn't take it all."

"No, you didn't, not this time, but you took more than you thought you could, didn't you?"

"Yes. You are a big man, Daddy."

He chuckled and gave her a kiss on her forehead. "Yes, but that was just one example of being able to do more than you thought you could. I'm sure you were quite leery about anal play and yet you gave the most incredible moans when I slid my fingers into your ass. You also didn't believe you were multi-orgasmic and yet you came not once, not twice, but three times under my mouth and fingers."

"I-I still can't believe I did that," she admitted, the heat settling between her legs, causing a trickle of moisture to slip along the seam of her pussy.

"You are more capable than you think. You are far more of a sexual creature than you allow yourself to believe. Trust me, Janie, I'm going to teach you things you've never imagined, have you flying apart too many times to count, have you sobbing in contrition when I've had to blister your little bottom, but I swear to you, you will never have to worry that I'll push you too far."

"I-I believe you, Daddy."

"Thank you, and might I say that every single time I hear that word from your lips, it makes me feel honored?"

"It just feels right," she said honestly. "I didn't think it would, or that it would feel fake or something, but, it doesn't. I-I really like saying it."

"Good because I love hearing it. Is there anything besides diapers, bottles, or pacifiers that you object to?"

"I don't want to crawl around or have to talk like a baby. I didn't think I'd want to ever wear Little clothing, but those women at the doctor's office were and they didn't look weird... but I guess maybe some people would think they did. It's all a bit confusing, and I guess I'm not real sure what I will object to."

"Then how about we leave it to explore? We can go shopping for some things, and you can wear them either when we are at home or perhaps to a play party. How does that sound?"

It sounded both lovely and a bit scary. "You mean where other people could see me as a little girl?"

"Where other daddies and mommies attend with their own little ones," he agreed. "Where no one would judge you or think you or our dynamic is weird. You saw some of those couples at Dr. Harper's and, in fact, have known a couple for some time now."

That had her sitting up straighter. "Who?"

He grinned. "How do you think I found you?"

"Are you saying that Mr. Lawson is a daddy? I knew it!" she said, practically bouncing on his lap. "His wife is just so pretty and sweet!"

"Yes, but, believe me, she is also quite a handful. She was actually supposed to dine with us that evening, but had misbehaved. Instead of going out, she spent her evening facing the corner while writing a long essay on how a little girl should not backtalk her daddy."

"Oh," Jane said as she pictured the beautiful woman she'd often served at the restaurant doing such a thing. "Do... do they go to these parties?"

"Yes, as do several other couples whom I can't wait to introduce you to."

Nodding, her tummy flipping at the thought of meeting others like her… women who enjoyed both being adults and being a Little was exciting. "I think I'll like that, Daddy. Oh, wait, there isn't any… any spanking at these things, is there?"

He laughed, hugging her close. "Only on the bare bottoms of little ones who decide to be naughty," he said, causing her tummy to feel as if an entire room full of little girls was doing somersaults inside it.

"Then I'll just be really good," she said, giving him a frown when he just laughed again. "Hey, it's not funny."

"I'm not laughing at you, sweetie," he said. "I'm laughing at the fact that you actually seem to believe that."

"I do!"

"Really? Aren't you the same little girl who tested her daddy at the doctor's office? The same precious girl who just had to see if she could believe what her daddy had said?"

"Oh… well, yes, but…"

"Exactly," he said, giving her bottom a pat. "Your panties will be pulled down and your butt bared and paddled if you are naughty, no matter if it is in the middle of the doctor's office or the middle of a party. Understand?"

"Yes, sir," she said softly and then smiled. "I guess I'm going to have to buy some cute panties… you know, just in case."

This time when he laughed, she joined him, already wondering what it would be like to have an entire room of people watching her being instructed to lower her panties so that her daddy could redden her bottom. Just considering it had her having to squeeze her thighs together a little tighter. How she had gone from innocent and curious just days ago, to a woman already spanked, whipped, face fucked, and made to come repeatedly, she didn't know, but damn, she was happy she had.

CHAPTER THIRTEEN

Sawyer enjoyed watching her expressions as he gave her a tour of the apartment. When she pressed her hands and nose up against the glass wall, he instantly imagined her doing so, naked, her nipples puckered against the cold glass as he took her from behind. Her eyes were huge as he led her into the master suite, the king-size bed with four posts on the corners reaching toward the tall ceiling, and he once again imagined her spread-eagled in the center, each of her limbs tied to a post, her body open and inviting him to send her flying yet again. The vision of her body bent over the ottoman in front of the fireplace, the flames flickering and sending shadows dancing across her skin as he laid stripes across her naughty ass before plunging himself into her, had his cock stiffening. He could easily picture her in the huge tub, bubbles covering her from his view and yet he would still enjoy every inch of her as he washed her, lifting her dripping form from the water, fluid sluicing off her body and yet more moisture gathering between her thighs, knowing that her daddy would soon be taking her to heights she'd never imagined.

They ended the tour in his office; a large room that he used far more often than the formal living room where they'd begun.

"This is amazing," she said, spinning around as if afraid she'd miss something. One wall contained nothing but floor-to-ceiling windows, his desk sitting in front of the expanse of glass. This was another piece of furniture he could easily see her bent over, her bottom bared, her lip trembling as he reached into the drawer to remove a wooden ruler, or plucked a length of rattan from the crock that sat within easy reach. He'd run a hand across her quivering flanks, giving each lobe a squeeze as he chastised her, letting her know that she'd soon be a very contrite little one as he lifted his arm to apply ruler, paddle, cane, belt, or hand to her beautiful plump ass.

She walked to the opposite wall where bookshelves were filled with hundreds of tomes. Everything from nonfiction biographies, books pertaining to business dealings, the latest bestselling fiction were interspersed with classics and books of erotica. Several ageplay books were sandwiched between bookends that were large brass teddy bears. He watched her smile as she stroked a finger along a book's spine.

"You're free to choose whatever you'd like to read," he said, joining her. "I'll ask that you read a certain few in order to better understand our chosen dynamic, but anything else you'd like to read, please feel free."

"This is a lot of books," she said, looking up at him. "I have a ton of digital books on my Kindle, but I do love curling up with a real book too."

He smiled. "Then we have that in common as well." When she began to pull a book from the shelf, he shook his head. "But first, we need to finalize our agreement."

She slid the book back into place, giving it a look of longing but allowed him to take her hand and lead her to the desk. Taking a seat, he pulled her down onto his lap before opening a drawer and pulling out several sheets of paper.

"This is the same agreement that we began on the computer. And while we've already begun our journey, I want to go over it again and complete the forms."

She nodded and he went through each page, adding a few notes for clarification.

"Wait, this states we live together," she said, her finger running under a line of script. "I-I can't do that."

"Why not? We've discussed the importance of total immersion."

"I know, but what about Sarah? I can't just move out and leave her stranded."

"Jane, I'm afraid I'm going to have to insist on this. I'll be glad to pay your share of the rent until she can find another roommate."

"No, I mean, I can't ask you to do that. I-I guess I can take some money out of savings for a while."

Sawyer shook his head. "No, that is my responsibility as your daddy. You've saved that money, and I won't have you spending it when I can easily afford to take care of you."

Just as he had done, she shook her head. "I've saved it for school and... well, I want to go. If we do this, are you going to expect me to just sit around here, waiting for you to come home? I don't want to do that, Sawyer. I've worked too hard to let go of my dream. Not when I've almost got enough to enroll for the next semester. Oh, and work! I can't quit. Mr. Arturo gave me two weeks but then I have to go back."

"Of course you can go to culinary school if that is what you want," he assured her. "I'm not asking you to give up your dream, Jane. I'm simply helping you to realize another as well. I'll make up for whatever funds you lack. You don't have to return to work—"

"I do!" she interrupted. "I want to do this on my own. I need to do this by myself. I just need to work a bit longer, and I owe it to Mr. Arturo. He already said that when I graduate, he'd hire me as a chef. I want to start somewhere that I'm familiar with, with chefs who can continue my education."

"If you won't allow me to make up the difference, then

that is what we'll do. I understand the drive to succeed on your own and applaud you for it. However, I insist on you moving in with me and allowing me to pay for your rent at Sarah's. And once you've earned enough for tuition, you will not work until you graduate. I don't want you to run yourself ragged. I'm certain that Arnold will not only understand, but that he'd agree with me."

She hesitated, but finally nodded. "All right, but... what if we don't work out? What if I'm not enough for you? I told you I'm not very experienced and, well, I don't have a very good track record with relationships."

Cupping her face, he bent to kiss her. "I have absolutely no doubt that we will work out. You are perfect for me, and I already can't imagine life without you. Trust me, Janie. Trust me to care for you, to help you, to love you like you deserve. Can you do that?"

"I-I can try."

"Then that's all I can ask, but know that I'm hoping one day you realize that you are exactly where you need to be, with the one man who will make sure you are happy in all ways."

He flipped to the last page of the contract and handed her a pen. "Sign, Janie. Give yourself the permission to become everything you've wanted for so long."

She signed and after he had done so, she lifted her arms to wrap around his neck. "Thank you, Daddy. I really will try to be your perfect Little."

"Baby girl, I'm not asking or even expect you to be perfect. No one is. But thank you for trusting me." He kissed her long and hard, releasing her to grin. "Besides, if you were perfect than all those erotic scenes I've been imagining where you are promising to be my good girl as I stripe your bottom are for naught."

Giggling, she squirmed on his lap, pressing down against his growing erection. "I'm not very good at being perfect, Daddy."

Laughing, he kissed her again, patted her bottom, and

then set her off his lap. "How about we clean up and do some shopping before going to your place to get your stuff?"

"That sounds like fun," she said. "I'll meet you in the bathroom."

She took off running, and he opened the drawer to slip the contract inside. Closing it, he opened the middle drawer, his fingers running over the ruler as he smiled. Yes, he'd definitely be having her bring him the wooden implement after which he'd tap it against his palm, instructing her to lower her panties and bend over the desk. Closing the drawer, he stood. There was plenty of time to shower and quite possibly to fuck her for the first time before taking her to shop for some 'cute' panties that would hug that adorable little ass of hers.

• • • • • • •

Jane was halfway down the hall when she suddenly changed direction. Running through the living room, she came to a stumbling halt as she entered the kitchen.

"Oh!" she blurted, the sight of Sawyer's driver sitting at the table, rooting her feet in place. She tried to tug down the shirt that already hung to her knees.

"Hello again, Miss Jane," Richard said, setting down the sandwich he'd been eating and giving her a smile. "Have you met my wife?"

Jane's eyes flew to the woman who stood at the sink, elbow deep in soap suds.

"Oh, I'm sorry," Jane said. "We shouldn't have left the kitchen in a mess. I-I can do those."

The older woman smiled as she dried her hands on a cloth and came toward her, hand extended. "Nonsense, it's my job. My name is Gloria."

Jane shook her hand and then felt her entire body heat as she realized that the clothing she'd come in to get had to have been seen by the couple. God, her panties… her bra…

both had been tossed aside. Releasing the woman's hand, she edged toward the center island, refusing to look at the spot where she'd lain, where her daddy had used his mouth and fingers to make her fly apart.

"Um... still, I should clean up," she said, her eyes raking across the floor once then again, only to discover that not a single article of clothing was to be seen.

"Janie?"

Twirling around, she saw her daddy entering the kitchen.

"Did you get lost, baby girl?"

"No... I-I just..." Words deserted her as she imagined what the couple must be thinking as she stood there in his shirt and he stood bare-chested as if nothing at all was unusual.

"Are you looking for your clothes?" Gloria asked.

Not able to speak, Jane simply nodded.

"They should be just about dry," Gloria informed her with a smile. "I'll go check them."

Jane could only nod again, wishing she was anywhere else but standing half naked before them.

"That's okay, Gloria," Sawyer said, taking Jane's hand. "I'll grab them. Oh, and Richard, can you bring the car around in a half-hour or so? We are going to shower and then do some shopping."

"Certainly, sir."

"It was a pleasure to meet you, Jane," Gloria said, giving her another smile.

"Oh... nice to meet you too," Jane managed, wondering if the woman knew it was a blatant lie. Sawyer led her across the kitchen and through a door on the other side. The moment they were alone, she released his hand, wrapping her arms around her middle, and moaned. "They know!"

"Know what?"

"Sawyer! They saw my clothes all over the floor! They have to know you... you did that to me. In the kitchen! Oh, God, I'm going to die of embarrassment."

He chuckled, his arm tightening around her waist. "No,

you're not, and, baby girl, don't worry. You couldn't meet nicer people, neither of whom have a judgmental bone in their bodies." Opening the dryer, he removed her skirt, folding it before reaching back inside for her blouse. Ducking between him and the dryer door, she yanked her underwear out, waving both items in the air as she said, "They saw my panties! They know I'm naked!"

"Baby, you are not naked, and even if you were, they wouldn't bat an eye. You don't need to worry about a thing." He took her undergarments from her and added them to the pile.

"How can you say that!" she hissed and then stiffened. "Wait. How many other women have you paraded through here? How many other women have dropped their panties or worn your shirt?" Her voice was shrill and yet she couldn't seem to stop. "How many other sluts have you fuc... had sex with on the counters!"

"Janie, calm down," he said. "I don't appreciate your tone, and while I'm glad to see you managed to catch yourself before you cursed, I certainly don't appreciate you demeaning yourself."

"No? So only you can demean me?"

His answer was to place her clothing on top of the dryer, slip an arm around her waist, and apply his hand to her butt... hard. The swat caused her to yelp and go up onto her toes. The second caused her to squeal, the third and fourth had her dancing in place, wagging her butt up and down as if to throw off his aim. It didn't work as the next two landed perfectly across her butt.

"I will never demean you, young lady, and you won't be allowed to either. You are not a slut. You are my little girl and not a soul in this household will ever think you are anything but loved." Another swat had her eyes welling as she clung to him. A final one had her shame turn from being discovered in his shirt to shame at acting like a horrid child.

"I'm sorry, Daddy! I-I just didn't know what to... to think."

He hugged her close, holding her against his chest. "I know, but, baby, you need to stop worrying about what people think. There is nothing wrong with you and nothing shameful about two people making love. And, if you'd given me a chance, you'd know that Richard and Gloria understand completely as they have been living a D/s relationship their entire married life."

"They... they have?"

"Yes. I told you that you'd never have to fret and I meant it. Now, are you ready to be my good girl or does Daddy need to lift that shirt and turn your bottom red?"

She dropped a hand behind her, rubbing furiously. "I'm pretty sure it's already red, so no, thank you. I'll be good."

He chuckled, dropped a kiss on top of her head, and picked up her clothes again. "Good girl." Taking her hand, he led her back through the door where she managed to give the couple a smile. It helped to know that they understood the dynamic, but she still prayed that her daddy had invested in soundproofing every room in the penthouse and hoped that there was no evidence of her spanking visible through the white cloth that brushed against her ass with every step.

His shower was huge and sharing it with him was an experience she'd never tire of. He soaped every inch of her body, his hands running over every curve and fingers dancing along every nook and cranny of her cunny. She shuddered as he instructed her to bend forward, his fingers pulling one globe of her ass away from its twin in order to scrub her cleft and bottom hole.

"I'll be filling this before we go," he said, pressing against her pucker with the pad of his finger. "A nice plug will go a long way to remind my little one that she is not to throw a fit, don't you think?"

"I-I... I don't know, Daddy," she said, her bottom instantly trying to clench at the very thought of being filled.

"Well, I do," he said in a tone that brooked no nonsense. "Tilt your head back and close your eyes while I wash your hair."

She obeyed and moaned as strong fingers massaged her scalp. It felt fabulous but not as wonderful as when he finally turned her to face him, allowing her to run her hands over his naked body. He was truly magnificent. His shoulders were broad and his chest hard. Muscles were defined in his abdomen and she had to bite her lip to keep a moan at bay as she encircled his cock with her fingers, lifting it to wash gently. It was like she was in a trance, fascinated at the very size of him, the weight of his shaft in her hand, the memory of his cockhead battering the back of her throat blooming in her mind. What started out feeling like the softest velvet soon became a rod of steel as she stroked her hand up and down its growing length.

"Baby, unless you plan on having me wash you all over again, I suggest you stop."

"Oh!" she said, jerking her hand away. "I-I'm sorry."

"Don't be," he said, reaching to tilt her chin up with his finger. "I was planning on taking you in bed for the first time, but I have no problem changing my plan."

It took her a moment to process his hint and then she smiled, moving to press her wet breasts against his slick chest, giving him a hug before she slowly turned around. Placing her hands against the tiled seat, she wagged her bottom. "I've never had shower sex before."

"Now that's a goddamn shame," he said, running his hand across her flanks. "Spread your legs and lift your bottom for me. Put your face down on your hands."

She eagerly obeyed and practically purred as he ran his fingers along her sex, spreading her labia open. Jane knew she was wet and not because of the water still sluicing over them. It seemed that just a look, a touch, a mere suggestion of what he'd do to her had her body instantly responding, readying itself for his possession. Still, when he replaced his fingers with his cock, she couldn't contain a loud cry as he filled her.

"You-you don't fit!" she said as her pussy stretched.

"Oh, believe me, I'll fit," he countered, his hands around

her waist pulling her back against him. "Every single inch of my cock will be buried inside your tight little pussy."

She was taught once again that doubting him only proved her wrong as inch by inch he sank into her. It was unlike anything she'd ever felt before. Every movement awakened nerve endings and set her body on fire. "Yes," she moaned, pushing her hips up, offering him whatever he wanted. "Oh... oh, God, yes."

Once he was balls deep, he stilled, leaning over to kiss the nape of her neck. When his teeth took a nip, she yelped and her pussy clenched. "That's it, baby, hug my cock. I want to feel your sweet pussy squeezing it as I fuck you."

And fuck her he did. He retreated and advanced slowly a few times, allowing her body to become accustomed to the invasion but soon he was pounding into her. He held her steady as he claimed her, each stroke having her give a cry, a gasp, a moan. His fingers fisted in her hair, pulling her head back, his mouth finding hers as he pumped in and out of her. He swallowed her cries, accepted her pleas for what she didn't know but he seemed to understand.

"That's it, Janie, come for me," he demanded, moving to nip her earlobe, her neck, her shoulder. She was attempting to remind him that she couldn't come from penetration alone when she realized that her body was coiling as he drove her to the precipice, and when he pushed deep, she learned that all it took to come was the right man. Her scream reverberated around the tiles followed by his bellow as his cock jerked again and again, filling her with his seed. The only thing that kept her from sliding to the floor was his arm around her waist... well, that and the fact that he'd yet removed his cock from her.

A slap to her ass had her yelping, her head turning back. "What was that for!"

"Some little girl lied on her questionnaire," he teased, still stroking inside her though she could tell he was slowly softening.

"You can't spank me for that, Daddy. I honestly didn't

believe I could come that way." He grinned and she could only giggle, not the least bit sorry to learn she'd been wrong. It took another quick wash before he turned off the water and wrapped her in a huge bath towel. She sat on another counter as he combed her hair and blew it dry. Every minute was enjoyable, from the warm air wafting around her to the fact that he'd not bothered with his own towel. The view was even more outstanding than the one outside the window.

Lifting her from the counter, he tugged the towel away. "All right, little one. Go bend over the bed for Daddy," he instructed with a pat to her bottom. "We'll get you plugged and then go look for some of those cute panties."

Blushing, unsure if it was with embarrassment or trepidation, she padded into the adjoining master bedroom and to the bed. Reaching it, she realized it was quite tall. Obeying him wouldn't require kneeling. Instead, she lay her torso down on the thick duvet, watching him as he walked to a dresser and opened a drawer. Her throat tightened at seeing the object he removed, his fingers running over it as his other hand reached back into the drawer to remove a bottle.

"Reach back and pull your cheeks apart."

She held her breath as her hands moved to do as he'd instructed. Gripping her buttocks, she pulled them apart as she buried her burning face into the duvet.

"Wider, baby girl. Daddy needs to see your little pucker in order to fill it."

Oh, God! His words had her body clenching, and she knew that he'd see that she was becoming slick… again. Pulling her cheeks apart, she also knew that he'd see the most intimate part of her wantonly displayed. She heard the sound of a flip-top being clicked open and then gave a startled cry as a stream of cold lubricant hit the cleft of her bottom.

"Easy," he said softly, his finger moving to spread the oil around her opening. "I'm going to push my finger inside

DADDY SAYS

to lube you. No, don't clench, baby. Relax and push back. You know you can do this. Let Daddy in."

It took all she had to obey, her arms trembling as she forced herself not to let go, to keep herself open. A moan filled the duvet as he slid a finger into her, her body jerking a bit at the invasion. He didn't scold her for the movement. Instead, he continued to slowly fill her bottom and then to rotate his finger, spreading the lubricant deep inside her bottom, coating the walls of her passage.

"That's my good girl," he praised, steady strokes in and out of her anus coaxing it to relax, to prepare itself for something larger. "Remember how Dr. Harper said that you'd need a bit of training before I fuck your ass?"

Yes, she remembered quite vividly and now that she knew the size of his cock, had felt it filling her mouth and pussy, she simply couldn't imagine it ever fitting into the small opening of her bottom. She didn't answer, but nodded, her face still hidden by the bedcovering.

"Well, this is only a small plug, but we'll increase in size until you're more comfortable."

"What… what if I'm never comfortable?" she managed to ask, turning her head to the side. "Does that mean you'd never… you know, do it there?"

"Fuck your ass?" he clarified, his finger sliding out only to be replaced by something that stretched her further. She knew it wasn't the plug as she could still see it in his other hand. As she groaned, she realized he had added a finger, two now demanding entrance.

"Ye-yes."

"No, it just means that I will take the time to allow your ass to learn how to open. I will be fucking your bottom, Janie. Both for punishment when you've been exceptionally naughty and for pleasure."

Hoping he wasn't expecting a response as she had absolutely no idea what to say, she simply turned her head again. Burying her face might not keep the color from rising to heat her skin, but it kept him from seeing how embarrassed she was that the very thought of having him push his cock up her ass, whether she liked it or not, had her insides tingling. Too late, she realized that he didn't need to look at her face. All he had to do was drop his eyes to look between her legs and see that she was growing wetter by the minute.

"Okay, little one. I think you're ready for your first plug." His fingers slipped out and after adding another dribble of lubricant, she felt the tip of the plug he'd chosen at her entrance. "Deep breath and then let it out slowly and push back."

Sucking in a great lungful of air, she began to release it, pushing against the plug, not to keep it out, but to open herself to its invasion. Still, she couldn't help but yelp as the tip began its progress into her. It wasn't as warm or flexible as his fingers had been. "Daddy!"

"Easy, Janie. You're doing great. Just relax."

"It's too big! Stop!"

"No, it's not. Stop resisting and let me in."

"I-I can't!"

A swat against her right buttock had her squeal again, and she learned that she could. It wasn't easy, but with her daddy, easy wasn't required. All that was necessary was the desire to fill her and inch by inch he did so. After a final push, he gave the plug a twist, as if assuring it could go no further. "Good girl. Nice and snug. Keep yourself open so I can wipe off the extra lube."

It took only a moment or two before he gave her a much gentler pat. "All right, up you go."

He helped her to stand and she immediately flung herself against his chest. His arms wrapped around her and his lips dropped to kiss the top of her head, something she had quickly come to love.

"You are fine, baby girl. I bet that you'll totally forget you're even holding a plug before you know it."

She huffed against his skin. "I highly doubt that, Daddy. It feels like I'm skewered on a telephone pole!"

He laughed and after giving her another hug, set her back a bit. "Babe, I promise, that was a little plug. Now, let's get you dressed before I decide to demonstrate the difference."

Her eyes dropped to his cock. Even at half-mast it was much larger than the plug he'd inserted. She didn't offer a single objection as he held out her panties, holding them until she'd stepped into them. Pulling them up, he patted her now panty-clad bottom, but didn't say a word. He didn't have to. She was positive she'd not be able to think of anything other than the plug, no matter what he'd said.

Once they were both dressed, he took her hand and led her toward the door. With a chuckle, he paused. "You can walk normally, Janie. It's not going to fall out."

Blushing furiously, realizing she'd been walking stiffly, clenching her bottom despite the fact that it only made the ache stronger, she forced herself to take a deep breath and nod. Besides, if she walked like she had been doing, every person who saw her would know that her daddy had plugged her bottom. That thought alone guaranteed she needed no blush of cosmetics as her face was quite pink already.

CHAPTER FOURTEEN

"Wow, this is so exciting," Sarah said several hours later as Jane and Sawyer entered the house. "I just knew you two were meant for each other!"

Jane returned her hug and then looked up at Sawyer. "I hope you won't be too upset, but... um, I've agreed to move in with Sawyer. But, don't worry, I'm still going to pay rent."

"Don't be silly," Sarah said. "I inherited this house and own it free and clear. All the rent you've been paying has gone for half of the utilities, property taxes, and food. The rest I've kept in an account for you. Now you can finally go to school."

"What? No, Sarah! That's your money!"

Sarah laughed and waved her hand, dismissing her concern. "Jane, you've been working toward your dream for a long time and, well, this is my way of helping. Look at it this way. The faster you become a chef, the quicker I'll be treated to a fabulous meal at your first dinner party."

Jane didn't know what to say. Never had she ever suspected that Sarah hadn't needed help with the rent. "Why do you waitress if you don't have to?"

"Because I'd be bored shitless without something to do, and I sure don't want to have to wake up early. Besides, how else would I get Brian's attention if I wasn't in sight on a consistent basis?"

"I knew you liked him!" Jane said, giving her friend another hug. "I'll make sure to invite him to dinner too."

"That's a deal. Come on, I'll help you pack." Sarah turned to look up at Sawyer. "I'm warning you though, you hurt my bestie and I promise you'll regret it. I don't care how big you are or how important. Is that clear?"

Jane watched, her mouth gaping open as Sawyer smiled and gave Sarah a small bow. "As crystal. I promise, I'll do my best to make sure Jane is happier than she's ever been in her life."

"See that you do," Sarah said sternly and then smiled and threw her arms around him. "I love this girl, so you better love her too!"

Leaving Sawyer to fend for himself, the two women chatted as they packed, Jane understanding just how much Sarah had believed she'd found her *One* because there had been a stack of boxes just waiting to be filled.

"I want you to know that I've never see you glow like this," Sarah said, tucking the last stuffy into a box.

"I'm almost afraid to stop and think," Jane admitted, sitting down on the bed. "What if I'm moving too fast? What if I'm not really what he wants? I mean, look at him, for God's sake. He is just... just perfect."

Sarah sat down beside her, slipping an arm around her waist. "What you don't know is that you are just perfect too, Jane. I've never known anyone as sweet as you. You strive to please everyone but yourself. Tell me, are you happy right this minute?"

"Yes, I couldn't be any happier," Jane said and then giggled and squirmed. "Well, maybe a bit happier if I didn't have this plug up my butt."

Sarah squealed and the two fell back on the bed in a full-blown laughter attack. It was several minutes before either caught their breath. "Oh, God, you are just adorable," Sarah finally said, sitting up and wiping at her eyes. "Dare I ask if the sex is as good as I think it is?"

"Now that couldn't be better," Jane said without hesitation. "Even the spankings didn't make me wish I hadn't met him. In fact, for some reason, they make me want to be his good girl, but I know that even if I'm not, he won't do anything but spank me and then forgive me. It's more than I ever dreamed of."

"Then, you have your answer," Sarah said. "Who gives a damn if it's fast? People spend years waiting as if there is one sure-fire thing that will assure they'll be happy with their partner. You don't have to do that as you already know."

Jane nodded and then gave her friend a long look. "But you want the same, well, maybe not the daddy part, but the rest. How do you know that Brian does too?"

Sarah grinned. "Remember how I said I was going out and not to wait up?"

"Yes, I figured you were just giving us some privacy."

"Well, that's true, but I also needed to answer that question. Brian took me to that club we kept talking about."

Jane's mouth dropped open. "You mean Silk?" At her nod, Jane lowered her voice. "How was it?"

"Fantastic," Sarah said. "Let's just say that I don't need rent money, but that doesn't mean I won't be having a roomie."

Giggling, Jane slapped her friend's leg. "No wonder you want me out of here. You need my room!"

"Don't be silly, girlfriend. Brian and I will share my room." Looking around Jane's old room, she smiled. "This just might become our own personal play space though. I can see a spanking bench where that desk is, perhaps a set of stocks by the closet. A rack on the wall for canes, hooks for paddles and whips…"

Jane slapped her hands over her mouth to hold back her giggles, but failed miserably. The two women hugged, each happy for the other. "We can get together and compare notes," Jane suggested. "I'm still discovering there is so much those books don't tell you."

"That's the fun," Sarah said, finally standing and pulling Jane to her feet. "You don't need books; you've got a hot hunk just waiting to teach you everything you could possibly want to know."

"And some things I'd never really considered," Jane said, reaching behind to rub at her bottom. They returned to the living room to find Sawyer who stood and took her into his arms.

"Ready to go, Janie?"

Sarah beamed and giggled. "Janie, huh? You've got a Little name!"

"I do," Jane said, "but more important, I finally have a real daddy."

• • • • • • •

After eating the dinner that Mrs. West had left for them, Jane and Sawyer decided it was time to go to bed… though it was not yet nine. She'd been hesitant to place her items among his, but he'd simply led her into the closet where she discovered he had made an entire side available to her as well as a built-in dresser for her folding clothes. Once that was done, he set her stuffies on a shelf of one of the bookcases that flanked the fireplace and the few pictures she'd brought were scattered in both the living room and his office.

"This is your home now, baby girl," he said. "There is nothing I'd rather see than the things that make you, you, surrounding us."

As they entered the bedroom, she did feel at home. Mr. Bear sat on a chair by the window, a quilt her grandmother had made draped across the back.

"Come here," he said, and when she did, he quickly had her stripped naked except for her panties. They were new, one of several pairs he'd purchased for her. "You look adorable," he said, cupping her bottom and drawing her close.

She leaned against him, her nipples rubbing against his shirt, the warmth of him surrounding her. "I can't believe you're mine," she said softly.

"Believe it," he said, bending to kiss her curls. "I will be yours for however long you'll have me." He paused and lifted her chin, tilting her head back. "And, I hope that will be forever for I can't imagine not having you in my arms."

She smiled and he kissed her, igniting her every sense. When he pulled away, it was only to scoop her up and toss her onto the bed. Bouncing, she squealed as she landed on her butt and the plug made its presence known.

"Um, Daddy?"

"Yes?" he said as he began to remove his clothes.

"When are you going to… take it out?"

"Take what out?" he asked, unzipping his pants and pushing them down.

"You know."

"Baby, you need to be clear on what you want," he said, his hand moving to pull his cock from his briefs. "Are you talking about me taking out my cock?"

Her breath caught as he stroked himself, her heart and her blood racing as her new panties became damp. That wasn't what she'd meant, but she certainly didn't mind that his obvious sign of arousal filled her with desire. When she remained silent, he tugged his briefs down.

"I didn't hear an answer," he said, beginning to walk toward her, his cock leading the way.

"Um… I meant… my plug," she admitted, wondering why she had to blush every time she said something the least bit embarrassing.

"Ah, the plug you've been such a good girl holding inside your sweet little bottom for Daddy? The one that I'm quite positive you never believed you'd forget about? That plug?"

Squirming at the truth of his statement, she nodded.

At the edge of the bed, he grinned down at her. "All right, on your hands and knees, head down and bottom up."

She scrambled to obey, trying not to think about how

she must look with her face pressed to the duvet and her bottom clad in her new panties with 'Daddy's Girl' emblazoned across her ass pushed up.

"Now, what is Daddy going to discover as he pulls these adorable panties down, I wonder," he said. "Besides a pretty little plugged pucker, that is. Am I going to find my little one's pussy is wet?"

"Yes, Daddy," she whispered.

"Wonderful," he said, peeling the panties down her bottom and off her legs as she lifted each knee. "Spread."

She obediently repeated her actions of earlier, holding her cheeks open, gasping as he worked the plug from her bottom, then moaning when his finger immediately took its place. "Good girl," he said. "You're learning to open. A few more sessions with bigger plugs and I'll soon be filling this little hole with my cock, won't I?"

"Ye-yes, Daddy," she said, no longer as worried about the inevitable, wanting to feel him taking possession of her last virginity.

He played with her pucker a few minutes longer, assuring her pussy continued to moisten and her clit to swell. She expected him to enter her from behind as he had in the shower, but after removing his finger, he bent to place a kiss on each of her cheeks and then pulled her up, holding her against his chest as he raked the covers back.

"In you go," he said, releasing her to climb between the sheets before joining her. He kissed her deeply and then slowly dragged his lips down her body, lingering on each of her breasts, laving and suckling on her nipples until she was writhing, her legs spreading, her hips lifting, silently begging him to enter her.

"Such an eager little one," he teased, moving down to kiss her stomach, running his tongue around her navel before dipping inside. She arched her back at the sensation, her nipples growing even tighter. Her pussy received its own kisses, its own swipes of his tongue and when he slid his hands beneath her ass and lifted her, taking her clit between his lips, she grasped the sheets and began to plead.

"Please, please, Daddy... I-I need to come!"

"Not yet," he said, his breath wafting across her throbbing clit.

"I have to!" she cried, her body ready to explode, her hips lifting higher.

"Daddy said not yet," he reminded, giving her bottom a squeeze. "Do you need help in obeying?"

"Yes!" she said, sure she'd not make it another second.

His first slap against her sex shocked her, the second had her squeal, and the third had her moaning. If this was supposed to be punishment, she would never voice the fact that all it did was ratchet up her need to come. That was until he grinned and the next swat had her eyes flying wide and her squeal becoming a yelp.

"See the difference?" he asked, his hand cupping her mound. "Funishment versus punishment?"

"Ye-yes."

"Do you need another swat before you are my good girl?"

Her head tossed on the pillow. "No, Daddy. I-I'll be good."

He smiled, gave her cunny a squeeze and then lowered his head again. It was hard and she did feel greedy as he'd already made her come several times that day, but with every lick and nibble, she had to fight against disobeying him. Finally, when her entire body was quivering and she was afraid she'd rip a hole in his sheets, he lifted his head.

"I love it when you tremble, when you make those needy little moans," he said, moving up her body. "And I love it when you scream my name. Come for me, Janie." With a single thrust, he buried himself in her and with another, his name echoed around the room.

"And Daddy can't tell you how much he loves feeling your tight little cunny hugging his cock as he fucks you," he said, dropping his mouth to hers as she continued to contract around him while he pumped in and out of her.

She didn't know how he held back, but she came again before he began to thrust harder, pushing one of her legs up so that her knee was at her shoulder in order to go deeper, pinning her down as he took his own pleasure—pleasure she so wanted to give him in return for the incredible gift he'd given her. Her hands roamed his chest, his shoulders, tangled in his hair, holding him tight as he gave a final thrust and released deep inside her.

When he pulled back, he smiled. "And I love it when my little one has to be reminded to breathe."

She inhaled loudly, filling her lungs. "I can't help it. You make me feel so loved, so treasured… knowing you're my daddy leaves me breathless."

EPILOGUE

Jane looked out at the door from the kitchen at the guests gathered in Arturo's. It was the same restaurant and yet everything was different. Tonight she wasn't serving. The temporary wait-staff had been hired for the night, allowing her friends to attend the party where the food served had been prepared by her. It had been a year of change, one that had offered her so many challenges, times when she'd doubted herself, sure she had bitten off more than she could chew. But every time she'd faltered, her daddy had been there.

The day he'd entered the penthouse and found her sitting on the kitchen floor, sobbing because the fourth soufflé she'd attempted had failed, he'd immediately sat down beside her, pulling her onto his lap until she calmed. With gentle words of encouragement and a kiss, he'd convinced her to try again. As she'd gathered fresh ingredients, he'd cleaned up the huge mess she'd made while she cooked. This time the soufflé was perfect and she'd beamed when he pulled out his phone to record what he called 'culinary perfection'. After snapping the picture, they'd sat out on the balcony, her again on his lap as he'd fed her each delicious bite.

It hadn't all been so lovely. The day he'd entered to see her waving a knife in the air and heard her screaming obscenities over the impossible expectations of her teacher, having to duck to avoid being hit by the tomatoes she'd thrown, he'd taught her that wooden spoons were not just meant for stirring. Despite the throbbing all across her nates, she'd still been seething. When she'd continued to curse instead of making an apology, her daddy had led her into their bedroom.

"Take off all of your clothes and kneel on the bed."

"I don't have time for a quickie. If I don't learn how to make perfect fucking knife cuts, all my work, all those years of saving won't matter. Is that what you want? To have me fail this fucking course so I'll be your… sex slave whenever you're in the mood?"

"Janie, you obviously need to be reminded that your culinary instructors are not your only teachers, nor the ones you truly need to be concerned about. Remove your clothes, get on the bed on your hands and knees, head down and that red ass well up."

"Why? You've already paddled me."

"Baby girl, I don't know what's gotten into you, but it stops this instant. Your choice of language and your continued defiance have earned stripes across that ass and, young lady, you're going to experience your first intimate punishment fuck as well. I guarantee it will not be a quickie though I'm sure you'll be wishing it were."

His tone, his stance, his look had told her she'd pushed a button she never should have touched. When she'd heard the sound of his belt being pulled from its loops, she'd forgotten all about lessons other than those given by her daddy. By the time she'd stripped, she'd been very sorry she'd not stopped her tantrum after the spanking in the kitchen.

The belt had risen and fallen a dozen times, each one leaving a searing stripe across her flesh. Her tears had soaked the duvet.

"I'm so sorry," she'd said between sniffles.

"That's a start. Now, turn around and face me."

She'd adjusted her position, watching as he'd removed his pants and briefs. Though she'd known what was about to happen, she hadn't made a move, having learned that she was to wait for his instructions. When he'd approached the bed, she'd looked up from her kneeling position.

"Open," he'd instructed and once she had, he'd guided his cock into her mouth. "I suggest you get it nice and wet."

Her lips had closed around his shaft, and her tongue had begun to lick along his length, swirling across the thick crown. She'd expected him to begin to thrust, to wash out her mouth for the vulgar words she'd uttered, but after a few minutes, he'd instructed her to release, withdrew his cock, and had demonstrated yet again that she was not the one in charge.

He'd patted the edge of the mattress, saying, "Lie on your back, pull your knees up, and spread those legs wide."

Once she had, mortified at the picture she must make, her striped ass burning against the mattress, her legs splayed open like a frog about to leap, he'd given her another instruction.

"You will keep your eyes on mine as I punish you. Drop them and I'll add a pussy spanking to your lesson. Understand?"

"Ye-yes, sir."

"Keep your legs open and reach between them. Spread your ass apart."

She'd hesitated a moment, but then obeyed, a bit startled at how hot her skin felt as she dug her fingertips into the cleft of her bottom and dragged her buttocks apart. The sound of the flip-top opening on the bottle of lube had told her exactly where her daddy's cock would be going. They'd been having anal sex for months now, and she had not only stopped considering it as taboo, she'd experienced incredible pleasure when he'd gently slide into her ass, filling her to capacity. But... that day, she'd known it wouldn't be the slow, soft lovemaking of before and hadn't been able to suppress a shudder.

"Please," she'd whispered. "I know I was naughty—"

"Then you understand that when Daddy says you'll be intimately punished, you are going to get your ass fucked hard. This will not be pleasurable for you but you are not to fight me, Janie. It will hurt, but I will not harm you. Understand?"

"Yes... yes, sir." She'd known that was the truth. He'd never harmed her. Hurt her, yes, as he was a firm believer that when punishment was earned, every stroke of hand, paddle, brush, or belt needed to count.

"Pull those naughty cheeks further apart. Present your pucker and ask your daddy to give you a hard punishment fuck."

"Please... please give me a hard... hard punishment..." She'd shuddered again, the next word she'd been instructed to utter the one that absolutely guaranteed she'd be sorry. She'd had no doubt that this time would be any different. Her eyes had filled with tears, not of physical pain, but at the knowledge that she'd so disappointed him.

"I'm waiting, Janie."

Taking a deep breath, she'd nodded. "Please, Daddy, give me a hard punishment fu... fuck."

"Where?"

Her daddy had taught her many things and this one... waiting patiently for her to fully acknowledge what was going to happen... what her choice of misbehavior had earned her, was one that truly allowed her to sink into submission. "In... in my bottom."

She'd watched as he'd applied a very small amount of lubricant to her pucker. Shame had filled her at having to witness his every move instead of being given the chance to hide her face in the duvet. When he'd slid his finger inside her pucker, she'd been determined to accept her discipline with dignity. After spending just a few seconds to spread the lube inside her channel, he'd tossed the bottle aside.

He'd moved between her legs, his voice stern as he said, "Remember, keep those eyes open. I want you to watch my cock sink into that tight little ass of yours. Put your hands over your head." Once she had, he'd taken her ankles and lifted her legs in the air, pressing them back toward her shoulders, practically bending her in half before spreading them wide. Moving forward, he'd placed his cockhead at her entrance. She'd barely had enough time to take a deep breath and push back before he thrust into her. Screeching at the abrupt entry, so different from that when he gently took her, she'd learned the definition of intimate punishment. The sight of his shaft, partially buried inside her most intimate opening had ensured her eyes slammed shut.

"Naughty," he'd said a second before she'd screeched at the slap he'd placed directly on her pussy lips. "Get those eyes open!" Once she had, realizing he had taken both of her ankles in one hand, she'd watched the other drop down to slap her pussy twice more. These weren't for play... each one had her cry out. "Are you going to be naughty again?"

"No, Daddy."

"What are you going to do?"

She'd understood he used these moments, forcing her to vocalize things that embarrassed her in order to focus her entire being on what her choices had earned her. Understanding his methods did nothing to negate the shame she felt at having to participate.

"I'm going to watch you punish me... inside my bottom." When his eyebrow had remained quirked, she'd swallowed and tried again. "I'm going to keep my eyes on your... your cock as you push it inside my ass and give me a... a hard punishment fuck."

Nodding, he'd again spread her legs even wider, making sure she had an unimpeded view of her intimate punishment. He'd pushed forward and she'd felt her body pulse. The pain had been sharp, her cry sharper as her sphincter had protested the need to open so quickly to accept his girth. Her daddy hadn't paused, and she'd watched his entire length disappear deep inside her ass. She had felt his balls slapping against her tender, punished flesh.

"What happens to very naughty little girls?" her daddy had asked, withdrawing until just the head of his cock remained inside her.

"They… they get puni… punished," she'd managed and then had moaned as he'd thrust forward again.

"That's right. They get punished." He'd withdrawn again, this time completely, which had made her shriek as her muscle was once again forced to stretch to allow him to exit.

"Please, Daddy, please… it hurts."

"Yes, I know. But, baby girl, that's the purpose of punishment. It is supposed to hurt to teach you to change your ways. Are you learning that lesson, Janie?"

"Yes… yes, sir."

"Good." Without another word, he'd thrust back inside her dark channel and had begun to fuck her hard and fast. Her fingers had gripped the duvet, her moans, gasps, whimpers, and pleas filling the air and yet none had swayed her daddy from his duty. She'd earned this. What had surprised her was the feeling of submission that had washed through her as he'd continued to pump in and out of her. The moment she'd stopped attempting to endure the discipline, embracing it instead, the sense of chaos, the feeling of being out of control had disappeared. When he'd slammed up against her bottom for the final time, she'd felt him filling her with his essence and had understood that, yes, her daddy was punishing her and not being the least bit gentle about it, but she knew that she was loved unconditionally.

After he'd pulled from her, she'd remained in position, not closing her eyes, not attempting to hide from him. "I'm very sorry, Daddy. Thank you for loving me enough to punish me and help me remember what's truly important."

"And that is?" he'd asked, gently running a hand over

her pussy that had been absolutely soaking wet in spite of that fact that it had been spanked, her bottom striped, and her ass thoroughly fucked.

"You… and me. Us. That is what is the most important thing to me. I love you."

Her daddy had smiled and moved to pull her up, her bare breasts pressed against his chest. "I love you too, baby girl. You're the most important person in my life."

After a long kiss that had her tummy flipping, he had set her on her feet, patted her sore bottom, and had given her a final directive.

He'd sat at the kitchen table, enjoying a glass of brandy, pointing out spots she'd missed as she'd stood, bare bottom as red as the tomatoes splattered on the wall, scrubbing up the mess she'd made.

The next afternoon, she'd become real friends with Gloria West. The older woman had entered the kitchen to see Jane studiously chopping carrots, huge piles of other vegetables waiting for her to practice her knife cuts. Gloria had started a large pot of chicken stock boiling, informing Jane that vegetable soup was always a great staple to have on hand. When she'd opened several drawers and rummaged in the utensil crock, Jane had finally made her confession.

"I-I um sort of, um, got rid of the wooden spoons."

"Ah," Gloria had said with a grin. "I tried that too, but Richard just bought several more and demonstrated the folly of trying to hide any implement by giving me a dozen swats with every single new one."

Jane remembered how her mouth had gaped open but when she'd giggled, Gloria had joined her and then had shown her a few tips on making perfectly sized knife cuts. Sawyer had come in, had seen the two slicing, dicing, and chatting and had smiled. That night when Jane admitted she'd discarded all the wooden utensils, assuring him that she'd replace them, he'd given her a spanking, but it had been one of the 'funishment' ones she had so come to love.

No matter what each day brought, he was always there, holding her close and assuring her that he was so proud of her, encouraging her every step of the way.

Tonight, she saw him seated at table twenty-three, the one that she'd always considered his since that first night of their meeting. He stood as she walked across the room and beamed as their friends who had been invited to help celebrate the completion of her first year of culinary school as well as her first solo service began to clap. She saw all the people she used to work with, Mr. Arturo and his wife, Mr. Lawson and Michelle, all smiling and clapping even harder as she passed their tables. Once she reached Sawyer, he pulled her to him.

"You did it, little one. Or should I call you Chef Knight?" he asked, brushing her hair back and running a fingertip over the embroidered name on her new chef's jacket.

Just like that first night, she felt a jolt of electricity spark between them, her nipples tightening. "No, not yet. I still have more to learn before I earn that honor. I'm just your Janie… and your little one, Daddy."

"But," he said, stepping back and slowly going to one knee, "will you also be my wife?"

She didn't even see the box he pulled from his pocket, or the ring nestled inside. All she saw was the love in his eyes a moment before her vision blurred and her heart skipped a beat.

His hand reached up to stroke along her cheek. "Breathe, Janie, just breathe."

It took her a moment, but she finally drew in enough air to answer. "Yes, oh, God, yes. I love you so much."

He slipped the ring on her finger and then stood, lifting her off her feet and twirling her around as everyone stood and cheered. Pulling her up his body until they were face to face, he kissed her. "Do you have any idea how happy you make me? How special you are? How very much I love you?"

She smiled and nodded. "Yes, I do because my daddy says those things to me every single day."

THE END

STORMY NIGHT PUBLICATIONS WOULD LIKE TO THANK YOU FOR YOUR INTEREST IN OUR BOOKS.

If you liked this book (or even if you didn't), we would really appreciate you leaving a review on the site where you purchased it. Reviews provide useful feedback for us and for our authors, and this feedback (both positive comments and constructive criticism) allows us to work even harder to make sure we provide the content our customers want to read.

If you would like to check out more books from Stormy Night Publications, if you want to learn more about our company, or if you would like to join our mailing list, please visit our website at:

www.stormynightpublications.com

Made in the USA
Middletown, DE
26 March 2024